Nude in Tub

NUDE
IN TUB

STORIES OF
QUILLIFARKEAG, MAINE

BY G.K. Wuori

ALGONQUIN BOOKS
OF CHAPEL HILL
1999

Published by
ALGONQUIN BOOKS OF CHAPEL HILL
Post Office Box 2225
Chapel Hill, North Carolina 27515-2225

a division of
Workman Publishing
708 Broadway
New York, New York 10003

This is a work of fiction. While, as in all fiction, the literary perceptions and insights are based on experience, all names, characters, places, and incidents are either products of the author's imagination or are used ficticiously. No reference to any real person is intended or should be inferred.

Library of Congress Cataloging-in-Publication Data
Wuori, G. K.
    Nude in tub : stories of Quillifarkeag, Maine / by G. K. Wuori.
        p.   cm.
    ISBN 1-56512-223-2
    1. Maine—Social life and customs—Fiction.   2. City and town
life—Maine—Fiction.   I. Title.
PS3573.U57 Q55   1999
813'.54—dc21
                                                    98-41977
                                                    CIP
                                                    Rev.

10   9   8   7   6   5   4   3   2   1
First Edition

For

GAYLE
WESTER
AND
CLAIRE

GRATEFUL ACKNOWLEDGMENT

is made for the original publication of the following stories, some of which appear here with a few changes: "Illusions" (as "Jim"), *The Gettysburg Review;* "Golden" (as "The Left-Behind Golden of Winter") and "Angles" (as "A Single Man at Sexual Ease"), *Literal Latté;* "Mothers" (as "Digby Fair"), *The Missouri Review;* "Skunk" (as "Rain-and-Patch and Terrible") and "Revenge" (as "The General Store"), *Other Voices;* and "Parents" (as "In Search of Anything Not Yet Lost"), *Prairie Schooner.*

CONTENTS

Quillifarkeag, someone once complained, is usually omitted from cheap maps. There is a forgiveness in the complaint that is not necessarily warranted. Quilli (as it is usually called) is not to be found on the more expensive maps either.

It is in northern Maine, this Quillifarkeag (kwill a 'far keg), what someone once joked was a U.S. protectorate tucked like a bug between the buttocks of Quebec on one side and New Brunswick on the other. It is both a small town and a township. As a township (a unit smaller than a county; the name of the county is Wulustuk) it also includes the even smaller towns of St. Antoine de Plupart and Quiktupac.

There is beauty in the area, where the tailbone of the Appalachians points a lumpy cartilage toward the Canada of the Gaspé and Kouchibouguac Bay. Potato fields spread a purplish haze in early summer, and the considerable acreage of broccoli, those stiff soldiers, is a richly green challenge to the toughest of winters—and the winters are tough.

To the west of Quilli by about forty miles is St. Antoine de Plupart (St. A de P to nearly everyone), a mean, gritty logging town that has retained the toughness of that crippling trade though the trade itself is now more of a machine trade than a man trade. The problem with machines, someone once said, is that when they break they don't heal. A wag naturally responded to that by saying that each time a man breaks he disappears just a little bit. There's always been a labor shortage in this part of the country.

Quiktupac, the outlaw town, is forty miles (or so) north of Quilli, an outlaw town because it sits on the border with Canada and has always been at the center of someone trying to subvert some law, tariff, or trade agreement by moving goods into or out of whichever of the two countries promises the greater profit. Many a youth has been educated at the small state university in Quilli with greenbacks pulled from cases of cigarettes or booze crossing the St. John in a canoe—usually at night.

A core group of Maliseet Indians live in Quiktupac.

They have a history that is as rich as histories usually get, one filled with the foibles, sillinesses, joys, and sheer meannesses that characterize most histories. Unfortunately, as Maine goes so goes the nation. The Indians are not liked much and it is because they are Indians. Good people in the area work on that, Caucasians (French, English) and Natives alike. No one has yet been very successful at it.

Quilli is also a state of mind, one marked by innocence and regret, by guile and sympathy. The people there will let you into their lives—but not very far. This has less to do with selfishness than it does with fear. Go too far inside and things start to echo, people get close. Honesty becomes negotiable. Bare all and someone still might say, "Were you naked or nude?" It's an important distinction. In a small place like Quilli the naked truth is hurtful. The nude truth is not so bad.

Nude in Tub

Land

GOLDEN

To die in winter in a far northern place is to become a storage problem. An uncomfortable building, only slightly heated, keeps the departed fresh for spring interment, although the affluent can opt for the dynamite and backhoe method of winter burial, not permitted in truly old cemeteries.

The early nations, the Wulustuk-yieg as they called themselves, who lived in the region (today) of Quillifarkeag and St. Antoine de Plupart and Quiktupac, had to substitute native genius for the booming thump of technology. As the stories have it—there is speculation here, extrapolation, though there is no shortage of evidence since those early tribes tended to be both wordy and a highly littering people—the deceased was placed on a kind of sled and covered with snow that was usually shaped in a rectangle.

Prayers were involved, beseechings to a spirit that

3

inhabited nuts and bees and reproductive organs and that governed trade with new people. Exchange of anything was always good. Had there been a stock market at the time and in that place it might have measured mood and persistence, ticked off chits calibrating desire and need. Perhaps that is what markets still do, the numbers being a variable translation of simple lust.

The snow was layered on as the rectangle was shaped. Each layer received several day's urine from the nation's women to keep the animals away. The animals did not understand trade, which is why, it was said, they were animals. Mourners could be seen over the lump at all times of night and day, praying and squatting. The golden block was then hauled to the cliff over the Pappadapsikeag River and pushed half the length of the sled over the edge. The calculation here was important.

More snow was piled on the rear of the sled to keep it weighted. In April, more probably May, the annual thaw, the golden block, gravity, and the river came together nicely in a clever equation of disposal as the item fell over the cliff, even though the nation had long since moved on for food or variety. This method

4

was surely complex, even lighthearted, since the Wulustuk-yieg were a humorous lot. As a nation, though, they were still small. Death was infrequent; thus, the complexity manageable. The ritual was thought to be fulfilling work.

Sometimes the higher layers of snow were shaped like eagles or caribou or—not always flattering—moose. In those cases it was up to the men to pee them golden. The women, presaging a more modern complaint, couldn't do it all.

FAMILY

It was an educated crew—that family—that went wild outside of Quilli, the man starting out as a professor at the tiny state university in town, his wife and four kids wanting to live out somewhere, way out, an old way in a new time.

"This is Maine," they said, and listed it all: heavy coats, woodstoves, lakes and rivers frozen by Christmas, moose, wolves, even eagles. The wife said, "I'm going to relearn French." The children went *Pow! Pow! Pow!*

DURING HIS FIRST DAY of staff orientation he was told: *Don't go living out somewhere. It won't be what you think.*

That afternoon they closed on a farm forty miles from Quilli, well beyond St. A de P. Leaving the bank, the man, Catullus Fender, bought the first ax he'd ever owned. His wife bought five kerosene lanterns and a kerosene can. Her name was June.

JUNE WAS AMAZED WHEN she told her oldest child, a boy, that she'd help him hook up the television and the boy said they—the kids—were more interested in learning how to chop wood and bring water up from the well.

"Let's get a book on plants," she told her husband, "and a book on wildlife. Maybe a book on the stars? I've never seen such clear night skies."

The next day, as Catullus was driving home from school with the books on plants and wildlife and stars that he'd bought at Don's Grocery in Quilli, he saw his oldest daughter walking alone on their dirt road. She was carrying something, or mostly dragging it.

"What do you have?" he asked her.

"It's a fox," she said. "I hit it with a stone."

"You killed it with a stone?"

"I strangled it while it was knocked out."

"Oh."

"Can we eat it?"

"I don't know. I'll have to look it up."

7

ONCE A WEEK THE dean would ask Catullus how things were going and he would say they were going fine. His students—the dean had heard this—thought he was a great teacher.

He had a full beard in hardly any time at all and June stopped shaving, too. Bit by bit, he told people, they were opening doors into the past.

JUNE WAS SCHOOLING THE children at home, which gave her comfort as winter came on. No bus rides into an icy ditch for her kids. Nor Catullus—he arranged for a room in Quilli with an old retired man named Bill. He stayed there only when the weather was bad.

When Catullus told Bill where they were living and that they were trying things the way they used to be, Bill, who was eighty-six and recently widowed, said, "Are you nuts?"

THEY LOST THEIR FIRST child that winter, an accident. Snow had banked up to the second floor of one whole side of their house. Their youngest child, a little girl, went upstairs and opened a window to slide down the snow. She closed the window behind her and took a great joyous leap outward and sank down into the fifteen-foot drift.

When the dean asked Catullus if there was any word yet, Catullus, as stiff in his face as a man with a beard can be, said, "She just disappeared. We think she was eaten by something. We've resigned ourselves to it.

That spring brought her slowly back to them, something noticed by their next youngest child while he was looking out a living room window on a drippy, warm day. She emerged standing, not even a look of fright on her face.

A small service was eventually held and they buried her on the farm.

The remaining three winters saw Catullus and June lose the rest of their children. Fevers took two of them, while the third cut off half of one foot chopping some wood and bled out while June was trying to remember how to use the cell phone Catullus had bought for her.

"WHAT CAN YOU DO?" the dean said philosophically. He could see the pain beneath Catullus's beard, but he had just told him he was being recommended for tenure and he hoped that would be at least a small bit of good fortune in what was an unending stream of hideous luck.

BILL DIDN'T THINK IT was all so sad, just bad planning, though he did say, "I respect your grief.

Catullus had just gotten off the phone with June and was certain that she'd gone plain crazy. She was cold, she said. She was freezing, she said. She was wearing every piece of clothing she owned, she said, but when Catullus asked her why she didn't just start a fire in the woodstove she answered, "I don't want to. I just want a switch on the wall, a nice little dial. I'm sure there's one here somewhere."

"FOUR?" CATULLUS ASKED.

"Four," Bill said. "That's what you said."

"Four kids—my children."

"Yessir."

"We had four," Catullus repeated. "That's right."

"You said like the old days, that's how you wanted to live."

"In a sense."

"Or lacking it."

"You're a harsh man, Bill."

"Oh—you know I'm not. Four kids?"

"As you have known."

"Just average, son."

"What?"

"Ten, maybe fifteen kids. Everyone had that, and everyone lost three, four, maybe five or more. You lean on history?"

"I teach it," Catullus said.

"You hit the average," Bill said quietly. "You just didn't have the whole team."

THERE WERE REPORTS THAT Catullus stopped June's suicide, and other reports that he did not. He was clean-shaven, though, when he told the dean he was declining the tenure offer, but Bill was the only one who saw him before he left town.

Catullus stopped by to pick up some books and to leave a final rent check with Bill. It was snowing as Catullus left, however, and even though Bill stuck his head out the door and waved good-bye, his cataracts and the heavy snow prevented him from seeing if Catullus was alone in the car or not.

He smiled when he remembered Catullus nagging him about the cataracts, about new treatments with laser guns and high-speed sound—whatever that was. Some things, he knew, you didn't mess with. You just let your times be.

SKUNK

Frank Terrible was an Indian of Maliseet descent, one of the tribal threads spun out of the old Wulustuk-yieg. A retired army colonel, now blind, he had, some said, fallen back to other ways, strange ways and unsettling, not what you would expect from a former professional during the years when he was supposed to be returning certain things to his culture.

Jenny Rain-and-Patch lived with him in the old Airstream parked in the center of his thirty acres. It was a brushy, woodsy piece of land near a small finger of the Pappadapsikeag River just north of Quilli. They had no driveway because they had no car, although there was an uneven line of power poles snaking in to the trailer because they did have electricity.

He'd taken the trailer in himself, pulling it with an old truck, a friend beside him, going slow enough for the trek to have taken the better part of two days, letting, he said, the land speak to him with its contours and bumps, nudging trees with little damage and backing up and trying again. He let the truck, he said, have a free rein, though he knew there were certain spots of progress where his friend's hand must have been dancing around the top of the steering wheel. Nothing tests a friendship like patience, he had said. "Besides, I could smell his arm."

In fact, the friend had steered him to a spot of some prettiness, a hillside with that piece of the Pappa and a view. Some said the friend had Jenny Rain-and-Patch in mind. Obviously, the only views important to Frank Terrible were his opinions.

JENNY BUILT A TOWER ten feet high and on top of it put a metal drum, purchased new, for their water supply. An electric pump kept it full from a hose leading down to the stream, and although some might have questioned their use of that water, in fact it was clean and caused no sickness nor threatened any future body lesions. Jenny, of course, had the water tested. She also built a rope-and-pole outfit that poked out into the stream so that Frank could go on his own to bathe or relieve himself.

Inside, civilization was a benign clutter with much of what they owned on counter and tabletop and any other handy surface. Jenny, raised mostly on city streets and in foster homes, found a certain strength in accumulation and its visible stacking. More than that, she simply never learned from anyone about tidying up.

They were an odd pair, as people often recounted it, yet a friendly couple who walked the roads for exercise. They also could be seen at any time of day or night since that didn't matter to Frank and since Jenny had never been in any place long enough to develop hard cycles in anything. They ate when they were hungry and often slept where they sat, sometimes governed by Jenny's impulsiveness and sometimes not. In summer she was, Frank said, like a fly in a landfill: nervous, skittish, delighting in every bloom or rodent that happened to stray into her life. Winters, though, pulled the energy right out of her and she would often sleep fifteen hours a day, slid sometimes half into the easy chair with her legs sticking out where Frank could, and often did, trip over them, or sprawled across the bed where he would have to move her around if he wanted to sleep on it.

DURING THE FIRST TWO years they were together, Jenny Rain-and-Patch brought up the subject of children no less than, she guessed, one hundred times. The issue was one of serious conflict since all Frank wanted was one good reason why they should do that, and all Jenny wanted was one good reason why they should not and Frank didn't have that, or at least nothing beyond the shrill and semi-ideological ideas about it being such a vigorous and careless world. Jenny had to move gently there since "careless" was of some sensitivity to Frank and the root of his adult blindness.

As happens with a lot of couples, though, the words became a soup of diversion and denial. Frank was afraid to sleep with Jenny because of her origins—all those years, she said, when she survived like a cockroach—and yet there was no way he could tell her that with all the debts he'd built to her since they'd been together. He loved her and he loved it that he had those feelings since so much of his life had been given to a cool and detached kind of attainment. He'd ridden a lot of affirmative action ponies proudly through thickets of prejudice, and while he'd been cut short of any noteworthy fruition, he'd been rewarded with benefits and security and had had to face the fact that if it had all been rather dull that was still pretty much what it was all about—except for Jenny.

THERE WERE TIMES, TOO, when babies had nothing to do with anything and Jenny simply wanted Frank, when there was too much to do in a day to worry about symbols in her head or to wonder that the ache in her body meant anything other than that when they were in bed, it would be good and there would be closeness in his putting it in her and no need to argue one way or the other.

She knew he was afraid of something, and she thought it was good to have some fear so that life didn't degenerate into nothing more than eating berries or sticking your toes into the stream or feeling the hot sun on your face early in the morning's cool.

Jenny relished their privacy, too, since she'd never had any of that, but she also relished their water arrangement and the electricity and the television and having mail coming addressed to her at one place over a period of time. The trailer, after all, was not a mud hut and they had conveniences and time enough to pick at their feelings the way some people pick at sores, and she respected that.

She was hard to pin down and she knew that, too, but it also left her feeling empty when she tried to figure out what it was he didn't like. She knew it was all in him so she didn't chew herself up about it. But every time she tried to bring it up directly he would smile and haul out something about spirits and bend her way around over that because she didn't know what he was talking about, thinking at first that it was old army stuff about dead boys and all, but for chrissakes he'd been an accountant for most of his twenty years in the army and as far as she knew the only death he'd ever seen was when the computers crashed.

Or else his lips would get real thin, about as wide as one of the deep lines on his face, and he'd talk about the search of his forebears for that terrible line that divided peace and war and for a place that was said to exist somewhere up there in Quebec, a reality, he said, that might even prove they were one of the lost tribes of Israel. Jenny thought he could only say that because he thought her a true fortress of stupidity and so they fought, words tumbling around like pool balls on a

17

table, blows deflected into irritations, Frank finally brushing past her to follow the rope down to the stream to take a leak.

SOMETIMES SHE PRAYED ABOUT things. Her own way, long ago, had been to find the middle of a street and walk down it, talking away and working things out, calling accounts to account, a woman with affairs in hand, no board to answer to or from which to gain advice and no creed getting in the way, but a rising going on nevertheless, a presentation, an accusation, maybe even a reconciling. After enough people had yelled at her with all the vileness car security permitted, she would find herself at curbside, calmed, in touch once again.

In this place it should have been easier since she had an outcropping of stone above the stream and a view, a clear ending of walls, and confinement and a clear ending of Frank, too: light, wind, sun, and silence, although from below there would be the shapes and shadows of faces staring up at her, a thing she knew about tricks of the eye and heart, a way the air had of seeming to be fluid, heavy, full of particles that, closer to the ground, turned into trees. She knew at such times that it was all Frank and she tried to put him aside, his needs especially, all of his needs, to go away and not trouble her and to stop thinking so poorly of her. If she was just a spot on his wall he could scrub her away and why didn't he do that?

Jenny didn't know what she was praying to at those times, or if there was even anyone who might call it praying, but the results of it were different now from what they had been only months before, the wash of clarity having abandoned her so completely that it seemed anymore like she did it only to scare herself. She would wonder why she was out here living in the woods with Frank, whom she loved, and who was one way of surviving, when there could have been many others. Sometimes she'd lie in Frank's arms all night long and he would whisper to her and be stiff as a drink, but when she'd try to squirm onto him he would always be maybe just another quarter inch away until finally he'd be up against the wall and snoring and soft.

She came upon the rock one day when she was up on the cliff and thinking about striking a line from the cliff to her water tower, a precautionary thing since sometimes during a storm there was a vibration to it that caused a worry. She wasn't concerned about any disaster even if the whole thing fell since it wasn't that big. It was just that she'd built it once and didn't feel like building it again if all the thing might need was a little support in a wind.

The rock was large and flat, maybe ten feet around and covered with a mossy beard. She found a smooth spot on it where she could lie down and stretch out, some flowers by her hips and within reach of her fingertips, the sun at the time hot, dizzying as the thick air seemed to pull her loose from everything, not just their property or the metal lunch box they lived in, but also her thoughts and her thoughts about her thoughts, all the brain gas burned up on Frank— lying there with that sun on her and feeling wealthy and idle and committed only to heat and time, deciding on subsequent days to lie there wearing only her underwear and to let the rock cook her from one side while the sun worked on the other.

Another day she took the mail with her and while she was tearing open a packet from some charity discovered two sheets of paper with stickers on them, animals like skunks and porcupines and raccoons holding up bottles of blood. She pulled off a skunk and stuck it on the center of her forehead, then put a sticker on each cheek and wondered how Frank would react if she became fat, maybe grossly fat, thumping wobbly. He did touch her after all and hugged her all the time.

Starting with the tops of her feet, she emptied the sheets of stickers onto herself, placing them in a patternless way and lying back to nap the way Frank did and the way he'd taught her, the way that had such devastating results in winter.

Her fingers brushed the plants and she pulled a blossom off something and stuck it in her navel as she drifted off, all of the sounds still with her, the birds and an intermittent rumble of wind, a plane overhead, the stream sounds below not fading at all, business as usual, even the sound of a car way out on the road coming through.

She wondered if they should get a telephone since the regular order of food they had delivered once a week from Don's Grocery in Quilli would have to be supplemented if she were going to get fat. You couldn't get fat on white bread alone and seven pounds of hamburger, not broad-ass fat with cliffs on her belly and slitty eyes. She had known women years ago who'd eaten dirt and they'd been fat and she supposed she could try that if Frank didn't think they could afford a phone. There should be ways to make it palatable, not tasty, not even good, only ways to make it go down and stay there.

Frank's unshakable tolerance would be twitted by all of this, of course. His faith in her might begin to sour. He might start wearing his bell belt again, which he did whenever his confidence ran aground, his way of seeing to it that every step was noted, his presence felt. He had tried to pull that practice out of the lore and mores of the native tribes but Jenny hadn't bought it. Frank so often used his heritage as a badge of abuse that she lost track of things she might genuinely be able to learn from him. Mostly, she thought, it was probably like living with a Catholic or a Jew, somebody harmless enough not to want to ram things up your nose, but who had certain parts that had to shape their hellos and good-byes regardless of whether they were coming or going.

SHE LIKED THEM, THESE circles of conscious effort. Her skin was pink but not burned or burning, the circular spots of flesh apparent enough in her whiteness, even on her face where the skin always seemed tougher, the result, she supposed, of years and years of grinding in the makeup.

While getting Frank's supper and chatting with him in a way that finally made him remark that she was acting pretty light for a change, she almost told him that she wasn't wearing anything except her panties and some skunk and bear stickers until she thought better of it, that he would take it the wrong way and shut himself up.

As she served him, she wondered where she'd put what was left of the junk mail. She always had so little that she never threw anything away unless she was convinced of its absolute and total uselessness for all time. That had been the way with the condoms, and she remembered throwing them away and thinking that it was all about consequences and if a baby came of that throwing away then it was time and a child would be welcomed. In the other regard, the one of disease that she'd learned out there long ago, Frank had simply been clean enough and considerate and gentlemanly enough that she'd had to force any thoughts of toxicity out of her mind while at the same time accepting that, if she was wrong, then perhaps there was something about a particular time in that, too, about a time when some people should not live to much of any age at all. It was all a good line of thought for a lovemaking that had never even happened, but, anyway, she had thrown the condoms in the stream almost two years ago and had been shocked when she'd found the bag not long ago casting out a reflection and catching her eye from within a muck of water junk. Without thinking that conditions had changed any, she'd flipped it out with a stick and back into the center of the stream.

"What are you looking for?" Frank called out. She was back in the bedroom closet where Frank had some boxes.

"Panty hose," she said. Close enough. "I thought I had some panty hose around here." For a moment, she stopped to think if he knew what panty hose were. He was only blind, she reminded herself, culturally diverse maybe, but not culturally dead.

"I have some extra socks," he said. "You may certainly borrow them."

"Childish things, Colonel," she said. "From another life. I have put them away, you know? But I have something to strain and I thought they might work."

"Berries?"

"Well—" She found it then, a box with three cans of spray paint and some tools and rope and a few small boxes of screws and nails. "No."

ON THE ROCK ONCE again, the stickers going back on in precisely the same places, she looked at the can of paint—dark green—and shook it, turning her head back toward home to see if Frank was outside. She didn't think so. She spritzed some paint onto one finger and then ran the finger across one eyelid and then the other, lying down with her eyes closed to let the paint dry.

How much longer could she go on eating hamburger and getting only love in return and the oddest sort of love at that? Love and maintenance, time—decency? He said he only wanted conversation with someone who didn't find a three-syllable word something for which to train. That's not, she knew, a bad wish, not blameworthy.

There were other things, too. Jenny had land with Frank, acreage in Quilli Township that he'd put in both their names along with the goddamn savings book, too. For a moment her eyes felt watery and she decided she had to stop this way of thinking or she was going to end up with paint on her eyeballs. Frank was fun, dammit all, playing his blindness like a harmonica and telling stories all the time, like when he went into a bar in Chicago once, before the blindness came, long before, and fell in love with a female impersonator, not knowing right away, of course, what she was.

"I was smitten," he said. "Yoked and bound into love's cruelest trap: the face, eyes of pain, a giggle, skin of china. Porcelain? But her face was this amalgam of all the cute girls I'd known as a kid, the earliest girls when I was still waking to all of it. Maybe it was her smell, possibly a perfume. But she had an oval face and a small nose and heavy eyes where she looked drunk or sleepy. We went back to her place and took off our clothes and there was this shyness—you know. Oh, yes. But my mind was planning trips to a store that was closed for inventory, the item still there on the shelf if the manager would only give me a minute. I had fallen in love with a face and could not put that down—my mind finally framing the thought, and I swear Jennifer, it really did, *She has a wienie*, and then began searching for a way to explain it since right there in a dim but neat apartment I saw, slipping away, oh Christ, Rhonda and Chris and Mary, older girls sharing my leisure but not my life—going, going, and as gone as a heartbeat."

It had been a scramble, apparently, of reclamation and desire. Frank said he wanted badly to cry since she was so perfect, but he ended up taking her to one of those jazzola places on Wells where they had a photo booth and had her take her pictures. Later that day, when he woke up sober and realistic, he looked at them again and laughed—not a lot, though—because she'd dropped her panties in the booth and those were the pictures Frank still had and that Jenny had seen, the girl or whatever she was hard and all but Frank still unable to throw those pictures away, throw that *face* away even if that face had fooled him pretty good.

Frank's stories were like that, Jenny knew, never just mishaps like how I got sick and threw up in front of a thousand shoppers in Marshall Field's on Christmas Eve, but rather how I threw up on this woman who was carrying a baby named Jesus, no relation, and so they went on like that.

• • •

THE STICKERS BEGAN TO lose their stickum over the next few days but they worked well enough. The next day as she lay down on the rock she took strips of electrical tape and stuck them to the backs of her thighs and calves. Frank's birthday was coming up, his fiftieth, and she was trying to think of something special she could do for him. It wasn't easy. Their lives were down to such basic elements that she sometimes felt like an old frontier woman: maybe put some special flowers on the table—not too effective for Frank —or make a blueberry cake or just spit on his hamburger. She had thought of removing all the lightbulbs and painting over the windows with the dark green paint and even painting the television screen, but she'd have to *tell* him about it and that would mess it up.

By the next week the stripes and spots were nearly complete and she felt good about the way the rest of her had tanned. With all of that and the eyelids painted she thought she looked good and she felt good, felt fine in fact, nothing inside acting untoward and Frank in good spirits, too. She'd been wondering how he might be reacting to his birthday but it had been a wonder and not a worry. She would have been surprised if she'd sensed some depression coming on or even something philosophical about the first half century or the first five decades or being only twenty years or so from the average death.

Birthdays, too, were hard for her to get into, since hers had never been celebrated, one of those habits that had never become habitual. She was glad, though, that it mattered to Frank, since he had talked about it. It just didn't seem to matter too much.

JENNY WAS SITTING ON the rock, taped and stickered, when the sun came up. The fog started to move with the rising heat, the stream loud and splashy with a whole weekend's rain. The morning chill had given her goosebumps and she was wiggling her toes and singing as she waited for the first light to begin warming her up.

Frank was sleeping late, having gotten drunk the night before on blueberry wine, a smooth and lightly sweet ferment that drank easily and gave a wretched hangover. Wearing the moccasins that he'd given her and the beaded loincloth, Jenny felt more and more a part of all this, something that she was supposed to be out here, singing like a zombie bird, humming

29

really since she could never remember the words to songs, sounds of lightness and good feeling falling onto her shoulders or into her lap along with the hair she was scissoring off, gathering it neatly as it fell and putting a stick on top of it so that it wouldn't blow away if an early breeze came up as she began to braid it.

She thought about the traps she had set out the day before and wondered how often she should check them, not that she didn't have time to check them as often as she wanted, but she had figured out that it was probably good to leave the various areas as undisturbed as possible. The traps should work well if they worked at all. They were just slatted and weighted wood boxes with a hinge and a catch and a ball of hamburger in the center of each. A small critter would be held easily while a big one could take the money and run and that was fine: she wanted a pelt and something to roast, not some cataclysmic struggle for survival—at least not her own survival.

Frank's portable shaver was in her hand and she began to buzz that over her scalp when the cutting was done, holding a small mirror up to check the work, noticing the line on her forehead where the tan ended and the whiteness began. She hadn't thought about that but it was interesting. She thought she looked a little like the man Bud down at Bud's Bar in Quilli—about two hundred pounds needed to complete *that* picture, however.

Her head felt cool and even the sounds of the woods seemed different. But after the sun had risen and had begun working around her stickers she reached up once and felt beads of sweat on her scalp and began thinking, *It's hot.* At one point she brought both of her arms up and over her scalp, her fingers dangling down toward her neck. Leaning forward, she rested her elbows against her knees, her forearms just touching the thin skin of her scalp.

She moved finally, the path narrow and rocky, descending rapidly and cramping her thigh muscles as she tried to keep her pace down. She was glad for the moccasins or she'd really have to be inching her way along. At one point she slipped and grabbed a pine branch and pulled her hand away sticky with the sap. Bending down, she brushed her hand into the dirt and remembered they had some paint thinner that would get the stickiness off.

Jenny heard the noise before she could even see the

small pond: unhappy sounds—rage, squeal, chatter, and roar.

She had come down to swim in the pond many times, her pond, damn, that was a kick, even though she didn't really like it and was afraid of it. The bottom was a sticking muddy and she assumed there were snakes in the water, snakes that bit, beady and blinkless eyes, awareness and nothing more, a grab for any motion at all or anything warm.

As she cleared the woods and moved onto the shore she saw the box some fifty feet away, such a primitive trap, just sticks and a few nails and some even smaller sticks stuck into some meat and holding the box maybe eight or ten inches off the ground. If the animal moved the meat the box would fall down onto its lid. Simple—it didn't take much. She and Frank would eat it and she would teach herself how to clean and work with the fur. Probably a hat first, since she had to make some effort toward protecting her now unthatched brain.

Frank was in such *good* spirits lately and he babbled on so, telling her how good she was and how she was so much of everything to him—although he seemed visibly to withdraw from her even as he said the words and Jenny didn't understand that. She thought she'd seen all the different shapes of pain and how people tried to get out of them but Frank kept on slipping away, all of his masks seeming to give a handle to whatever was hurting him, but if she tried to grab on to something, tried to work something through with him and get it out and get it away, he would just smile as though he were embarrassed in his struggle and he would try to bury her in endearments while Jenny seethed.

"Come on, wild thing," Jenny said. She was down on her knees some ten feet from the box, easing back on her heels and trying to match the animal suspicion for suspicion. "Come on, ugly thing." She could hear her own breathing and could feel the sun on her head and decided that a hat would definitely be the first priority.

It sounded like it was talking, finally, a soft, almost machinelike *yug-yug-yug-yug*. Animal, she thought, I am someone near and dear and someone to fear. Your instincts are working—as are mine. I cannot leave him. I cannot rid this neighborhood of me no matter how desirable that is because I have nowhere to go.

That's all. We all must accept me and deal with that, find a place: a brook, a hovel, a convenience store for hearts and histories not well controlled.

For a time Jenny had thought of pulling a tooth and wondered if she could do that. Odd deeds were becoming a snap, as was pain. Better to be a pig in pain than a roast on sale.

She stood and walked forward, the *yug-yug* increasing both in speed and pitch. Panic is a precious thing, little one, use it well. It's a fantastic fuel even though the price is high, really high.

It was a skunk.

There were two rages to be ignored and the obvious one was easier. She held the box out as far as she could with one arm, her head turned the other way. *Just do it. We can both handle it.*

It did, but Jenny ignored the steamroller going up her nose, concerned more about her eyes since it was obvious that this was a hard contest and a mean chemical and, shit, if they ended up with two blind ones down there in the lunch box something sure as hell would change.

The second rage was harder. Jenny had been unhesitant when she'd finally moved, putting her hand between the slats on the box and the slats on the lid and hefting the box quickly. The animal began chewing into the top of her hand and the knuckles. She tried stopping and shaking the box but there was too much life going on down there, so she just swallowed and blinked her eyes hard and stepped into the water, stepping high and wanting to move quickly, hoping the animal would tire soon or die of fright, but not many things ever died of fright, the pain nothing she couldn't ignore for a moment, like the sunburn she'd hurried too much into those first few days of trying to plan something for Frank's birthday.

The idea of that fury so close, however, was frightening, the fear and fury of total anger. Still holding the box in one hand, she reached down into the water and pulled off a moccasin, holding it against her stomach while she slipped her hand into it. She put her hand on the top of the box then and pushed, surprised at how the animal seemed to sense that that hand, all softly gloved now and not fisted in anger, was the killing hand. It seemed to explode at it and Jenny pushed harder, blood streaming from her nose now and she couldn't figure that out, the fury giving her the final grace because the animal breathed quickly and filled with water and died.

As SHE WALKED, SHE carried the box or, where the path permitted it, dragged it along. Already she'd looked at her hand and had been surprised that it wasn't shredded gore. Mostly, it was badly scratched and reminded her of when they'd first moved here and it had seemed like she couldn't move ten feet from the trailer without taking a bruise or opening up some kind of wound. She had laughed to Frank that the problem was her being a corner person and all, streets and angles and signs telling you what to do, and none of that was out here—too much unity from which she'd tried to stay apart until she got the hang of it. Someone had once told Jenny you didn't just go and live on the land. You asked permission first, became a supplicant of old mysteries and ancient gods. Sometimes there had to be sacrifices, appeasement—a question in any land. Joking, Jenny had replied, "That's why I have my Maliseet. He does those things pretty good."

Sometimes, she remembered, especially when she was teaching herself to do the firewood, Frank would rub her all up with liniment in the evening. No one had ever done that to her before and she'd liked that in him. Such things had not happened recently, though.

She made her way back to the flat rock, still catching an occasional jolt of nausea from the stench. Never before had she encountered a skunk, but, and she thought this comparison was good, it was like the first time she'd run into tear gas in the city. You knew it would be tough and it was and totally unlike what you thought it would be. But pain anywhere was always the same, making you breathe harder until you could figure things out, then giving you alternating stages of management and pissing panic.

Sitting down in her usual spot, Jenny reached into the box and pulled the animal out, flopping it down beside her so she could think her way through the gutting. The whole thing hadn't taken more than an hour, but there'd been a lot in that time to think about as well as things pointing to the future, too, things that involved more than just trying to find another part of herself to alter for Frank. She'd need a knife from the kitchen and soon so that's when Frank would know, at least if he was awake and she was certain he would be up by now—must be at least eight or nine o'clock—

although she wasn't going to say anything and she had to smile because it had just come to her.

A new perfume, Frank? Why—yes, dear. How sweet of you to notice. She thought that sometimes the remaining senses in a blind person just said fuck it and shut down altogether.

Smoke was coming from the chimney. Frank was up.

Happy birthday, she thought, stepping lightly and from rock to rock across the stream. She knew it would take a lot of washings to get rid of it, but she didn't want to get wet and diminish the smell. Not now.

"Hello, Frank," she said softly as she opened the door. He was right there, really right there, his face toward the door and he was very much naked and very much aroused.

Oh no, she thought.

"Come here," he said.

"I've had an accident—" Dammit and dammit all.

"You've done enough," he said. "Come here. It's time to stop it, Jenny."

Love

CONDOMS

There can be incidents in small towns like Quilli that make people think, and there can be incidents where thought is like the bad news people receive in thin letters. Where Alice and Fence were concerned, the business at the underpass was just nutty.

Not much was thought about it at first, since Alice Pawchawk and Fence Dzfru had been considered extreme people for a long time. Alice was thick-waisted and prone to hair, while Fence, everyone said, was wicked gorgeous. Green eyes on a man are unusual, and Fence was smart, too. He'd graduated from college in three years and had then taken a Dale Carnegie course, which nobody in Quilli had ever heard of until Fence said it was a lot like one of those Anthony Robbins things.

No one had ever heard of him either, but most people knew enough to shut up after getting two answers to the same question.

FENCE AND ALICE SOMETIMES painted themselves up all white—apparently, *all* white—which seemed odd, too, though they never left the house when they did it. Their minister, Jonah Donutt, stopped by one time when they were all white, and according to Jonah he'd hardly ever had a nicer visit.

"What did they say?" he was naturally asked by his wife.

"About?"

"About why they were all white, painted up."

"I didn't ask."

"Did they have clothes on?"

"White clothes."

"JUST A YOUNG MARRIED couple," someone said after noticing how Fence and Alice had painted their small house on the edge of town a rich, solid black— the windows, too. Everyone in Quilli knows how hard it is when you're just starting out.

"Just a young married couple," someone said, no doubt remembering how a young bride, anticipating children, will clamor and clamor for that first pet which, these days, seems usually to be a dog too big for wherever they happen to be living. Alice and Fence kept a frozen chicken—still feathered, eyes cloudy enough to make it look a little heartsick—tied to a rope on the porch just off the dooryard. Eventually they encased it in a fiberglass resin so they wouldn't have to keep putting it out and bringing it back in to the freezer all the time. The chicken had been Fence's idea, sensitive as he was to what people would think seeing a dog in such circumstances.

"Just a young married couple"—most people seemed to look upon that as a condition, something like the terrible twos or old age.

"I WOULD JUST LIKE to announce," Alice said one morning during Announcements at church, "that Fence and I are going to have a baby."

Heads turned, especially the gray ones. There were friendly comments and approbative murmurs about the population base in a small town like Quilli.

There was suspicion, too, well warranted, as Alice continued. "Tonight—we thought maybe baked with hash browns, some green beans?"

"Oh, Alice," their pastor said. A lot of people were

irritated, but they all knew the condition for what it was. They'd been young once, too.

THAT FIRST WEEK UNDER the underpass they did very little. Alice sat on one side of the road, Fence on the other. Eventually Alice crossed the highway to stand with Fence and they kept that arrangement. As cars or trucks came along heading out of town they would smile and wave, looking as though either they belonged there or they were just coming or going themselves.

AT THE START OF the second week they brought their twin La-Z-Boy chairs to the underpass and placed them side by side. Since they were just outside of Quilli they were of no concern to the Quilli day-shift cops, and State Trooper Val Dooble, when asked, said she knew of no state law that was involved and she wanted no more calls about it. They weren't obstructing traffic and they weren't being rained on. They were, they had told her, watching the cars go by.

Sometime in the third week two cots appeared behind the big chairs. At any time of the day or night then at least one of them would be sitting there, Alice occasionally working on her hair or doing her nails, Fence occasionally working on his hair or doing his nails.

"Public service," was the most frequent answer they gave when asked what they were doing. Mostly, though, they were not asked. There is hardly a greater sin in a small town than to be nosy.

Alice and Fence, though, wanted people nosy. They wanted them to open up and ask what they were doing. Being young was a performance and they were working hard at it. They wanted critics and public opinion, even suggestions. In short, they wanted to live the only truth that a young married couple can know: *Life is short. Be weird.*

THEY TRIED MAKING LOVE on the cots, but while several cars slowed down no one stopped, not even when Alice was on top of Fence and Fence was playing old folk songs on his harmonica.

They tried moving the cots to the center of the road, but people would just carefully drive around them, the more thoughtful ones tossing out a packet of condoms, both the male and female kind.

One woman, a passenger, handed Alice a small box of Ramses ribbed and said to her, "Safe sex. That's the thing."

"Ma'am?" Alice said.

"Yes, dear."

"We're in the middle of a highway."

"All the more reason, dear. All the more reason."

Alice gave it a lot of thought after she suffered a small vaginal tear due to some errant gravel.

THEY DIVORCED SHORTLY AFTER that.

"I don't know," Alice said, responding to a conversation about life they'd had. They had no car and were taking one of the La-Z-Boys home on top of a wagon borrowed from a neighbor's child.

"I don't know," Fence echoed.

Some people stared at them from the insides of houses as they walked along and they both knew they were being stared at.

"At least we're dressed," Fence said.

"Makes me a little sad," Alice answered. Fence looked over toward her then and smiled, a small wonder growing about whether or not he would marry again. "Life is short," he said to her.

"Be weird," Alice responded.

It's a tough burden for a young marriage.

NUDE

1

The car wreck between Quilli and St. A de P had been bad enough to bring the television truck up from Bangor, a four-hour drive over roads swollen with frost heaves and padded with old snow, ice chop, and ridged rails of hard pack.

Route 161 was the top of a T at the impact point, an old logging road ending at the highway. Beneath the logging road and parallel to the highway was a culvert, a steel tube that looked some six feet in diameter, a hard straw to help suck the winter melt on down toward the St. John.

Flanking the tunnel, the fenders and doors of the car were laid out as neatly as if a thoughtful person had put them there, while on top of the culvert on the logging road lay the roof of the car, all that metal looking bruised from the rude surgery but hardly dented and certainly recognizable.

Pearson, a man in his forties from St. A de P, with a need still to feel his own impact on things, watched the television truck prepare, watched the erection of the steel tower for broadcast, a young woman inside controlling that, a symbolism he could take to bed some night when he needed a few raunchy thoughts.

Pearson thought: Children have run afoul of negligence.

They had.

A tow truck was called in and while its winch had been able to shake the whole culvert with its tug, the car itself had not moved. Someone even said the heat of impact had welded the vehicle to the walls of the tube. A wait, thus, began for a bigger machine, something with treads to straddle the ditch. Pulling still seemed the way to do it since no one wanted to begin the awful process of going in with torches to cut the car out.

2

First on the scene, Pearson had known right away it was kids, could see that it was kids from Quilli. He saw motion in the car as he parked his truck and got out and slid and stumbled his way through the snow and down into the ditch, one child in the car visible through six or eight inches of rear window, or what would have been window had the roof not peeled like the lid on a can of chips, the car snugly reroofed by the sloping culvert.

When he first saw her she seemed calm, a sweet child, big silver earrings dripping blood from her ears, curly hair, black hair, a trillion curls he could see because she kept turning her head toward the side of the car, pointing with her forehead, mouth open *trying* to say something. Then she'd smiled and nearly broken his heart because he knew it wasn't intended, the smile working about the same way a broken bowel slaps the fright out of a person.

He leaned against the trunk, the top lip of the culvert near his forehead. Helping, even more than calling for help, seemed the more immediate need. Leaning across the trunk, he offered his hands—even yelling to get her attention—the window opening looking like it might fit her for exit, some luck needed, but then these kids looked like they were in line for some luck. She wouldn't reach for him, though, one arm held tightly across her chest as she kept looking toward the side of the car, her smile mismatched to the wintry horror in her eyes.

Pearson yelled at her again but that did no good, and finally she seemed to lean against the back of the front seat, her face almost lost in the shadow. Lying clear across the trunk and yelling once more—the car, he recalled, one of those old flatiron Oldsmobuicks—he finally saw her hand and reached for it off to his right until some minimum of thought in his head emerged and he realized she was still well into the car and her hand was over there, to his right, outside between the car and the culvert wall, her hand, the whole arm still in its denim sleeve, and he felt bad that he'd yelled at her, really bad about that. Finally, sticking his head into the window opening, he said, "I'm sorry."

Myrna had nodded, the proprieties of acknowledgment, of relationships, still working. The way Myrna remembered—she spoke to Pearson, her words about as audible as a snowflake landing on a stream, but Pearson did hear her—they'd all met at six at the shack on the St. A de P Road, had each drunk three beers—Had they had two cases? Where were they?—been at school by seven-thirty for the assembly, and been out at Remy's car by eight. It was what they did on Friday mornings, every Friday, like salesmen mak-

ing certain predictable calls. Talk had flown about dis-
cipline early in the year, but aside from the one time
when three teachers had *met* them in the parking lot,
threats of action had subsided.

Besides, everyone had known what they were doing
and where and when they were doing it and certainty
was a lot like forgiveness. Myrna said she had been
painting her nails in the car, had been holding her arm
out the window for her nails to dry while everyone
had been screaming they were freezing (themselves,
not Myrna's nails—Myrna laughed feebly then, and
Pearson felt his heart break), had leaned down to get a
can of beer, and felt her eardrums blow from the
crash. Her eardrums, she said, now that had hurt.

Pearson thought she must have said all that on pure
adrenalin because she faded then—nearly disappeared, though it was only death.

In the front and back, the other three children,
headless, sat, the heads on the back seat near Myrna's
knees, a hairy tumble of gore and sadness. The other
girl would be no problem, but the two boy heads
would have to be matched by someone to the two boy
bodies. It would not be hard. It would just have to be
done.

3

St. Antoine de Plupart had once been laid siege to by a gathering of Mieuq Macques, the siege beginning—there had been lots of time—with the laying of a ring of fecal matter around the village. Next, apparently, the Indians had found the settlers' horses a source of wonder and humor and had proceeded to cut the tails off the grazing beasts. Any wounds were packed with mud, which tended to mollify the anger in town, but not enough to prevent the townsfolk from urinating on the buried (and even hanging, depending on the perineal strength) food caches of the Indians when they found them. Escalation followed until one woman in town, a poet and marginal physician, dubbed it the Poo-Pee War. This tended to settle everyone for a time—even the Indians finding a crooked glee in their translation of the doctor's dubbing (*PaPa whoo'Sha*)—until a town boy found an Indian child firing off a salvo and kicked her so hard in the butt her spine cracked in three places.

That much was not legend. Both the doctor's diary and the record of a sermon confirm it. For the Mieuq Macques, a storyteller laid the incident out and passed it on until it found its way into a newspaper in St. Antoine de Plupart some fifty years later. As the accounts have it, the Indians had "enpumped that flesh all watery, when spewed then stoppered," then tied her with rawhide straps. All balled up—none of the writings ever mention whether she was dead or not—she was hung out during a "monstrum n'ester, think as cold plummets of th'effect."

It was said then that the troop moved on, leaving the child hanging in a tree to be "pissed own, byeten, eyeten, lance-ed" or otherwise abused by the unsporting and cruel villagers.

No such abuse happened. A smithy built a cage of iron straps that was hung from the branch with some difficulty, protecting the wadded-up child from vandals and most animals. The question arose from time to time over why they just did not bury it in the spring or summer and the answer was always the same: some variant of respect.

4

Pearson had always liked that story. It seemed, gruesome or not, a better way to treat children than what he'd just seen. The cage, he remembered, was still around. He wanted to see it, to make that connection to long ago because he'd never felt so close to madness in his entire life. He wished there were something easy to read about men going mad. Nothing came to mind.

After parking his truck, he went around behind the town hall, put his briefcase on the steps to the rear door, and continued on to the barn. Three padlocks were laddered on the heavy door, the locks brass and the door oak, the locks keyed to a key he kept on his own ring.

He hadn't looked up at the rear window of the town hall as he'd put his briefcase down, but he assumed Liselle was in there, near the woodstove, Liselle, who would have heard about the wreck by now and who would have spread a few things on of her own: kind chatter, concern, small handholds to climb out of a slowly shared grief. Another town was involved—Quillifarkeag, someone would have told her—so of course she would have be quite official, quite reserved, in her tellings, but Pearson thought the truth would all be cleaner if no one talked about it.

After keying the second lock, he turned back toward the town hall window and nodded once but didn't see any movement in return. Perhaps she was in the bathroom or perhaps someone was there: dog licenses (due now), delinquent taxes, even a complaint. They'd been out of salt and sand for two weeks so all they could do was plow and that was upsetting to some people.

Or maybe Liselle's daughter was there, Pierrette, seventeen, her hair the same ashy blond as her mother's but cropped down to a crew cut. Pierrette was pregnant but was still putting in a full day at the convenience store two doors down from the town hall. Pearson thought the girl he'd helped to die was about the same age as Pierrette.

He enjoyed his thoughts of Liselle, the first woman he'd ever known as tall as himself, a certain equality in height and a certain discomfort, too, as they shared an office built in a smaller time for smaller people. They tended to dance around each other but he loved those dances, insignificant times in a friendly place, grand frictions hip to hip in an unlikely boudoir.

5

Pierrette was at the town hall regularly and Pearson liked that, Pierrette knowing everything about everybody and telling it all not as gossip but as the most remarkable things about the *lives* of people, things she was told when people came in for their bread and cigarettes and dry gas and fresh hot coffee, not much ever happening to any one person—a spot of cancer (a northern ritual, common as potato blight), the annual flocking down the coast to Florida, the conceptions of children and then their achievements, car trouble, truck trouble, new cars, changes in transcontinental trucking regulations, the seventeen nuns down in Quillifarkeag, all, now, with HIV (a fiction, surely, Pearson thought), that old woman, not far away, who dug a hole in her backyard and buried herself in it—but all of it, fact, remonstrance, and anecdote, coming out of Pierrette like a single fine life lived well, nearly all of it recounted as she sat in the tiny bathroom near Pearson's desk, the door open enough that he could see her gesturing as she talked and tended to her needs.

He and Liselle shared that bathroom, an intimate haven of town property as clean and personal as could be found in any home, no roller towels or business air freshener purchased in bulk, no wall-mounted amber soap and no air dryer. They took their chances with cotton towels from Don's Grocery in Quilli and a big bottle of lotion. Sometimes Liselle would come out of there and return to her desk and sit down and run a gob of lotion into each leg, each shoe snapping off at the back so she could rub a little onto her heels. Her hands ran quickly and efficiently up and down those long unshaven legs, that hair like a golden highlight he'd once felt managerially responsible for, no reason given, until he'd reminded himself that she was the mayor and not he, and that while he was the town clerk none of that mattered too much since they both just did what needed to be done anyway, a conclusion he'd felt comfortable with even the one day that first summer—years ago—when she'd been wearing a sleeveless dress and had been reaching with both arms for a big assessor's book and he'd noticed she hadn't shaved under her arms either and he'd suddenly felt there were some things that a man, and not a woman, didn't discuss.

Pearson opened the barn door finally, clearly unsure of what had brought him there. He looked around and thought: we thus became, we thus became—all that death this morning was surely doing him in—in love, no, lovers, we were not in love, lovers scratched and rusty in an old cage right here in an old barn, our consummation beginning with rust-covered hands brushed lightly over a cheek here, a leg there, playful brushes over sweat-soaked skin, the cage having to be wrested from beneath and behind piles of century-old junk, wagon wheels and highboys, oak filing cabinets, pallets, and pieces of municipal memorabilia.

From out of all that they'd pulled the cage, the one that had hung from the tree for so long, the Indian child's carcass hanging inside it (not a trace now, but the impulse to look real close was always there). They'd crept inside it the one day to examine it for a use now forgotten, some naive fiscal economy. Too many pieces had broken away from the old rivets, the thing rattled and rolled with their slightest movement, and their movements were anything but slight after their hips bumped together and Pearson looked to see the hem of Liselle's dress caught on a piece of iron rust, her mayoral hips and thighs so close to his nose he could smell years of office fantasy pouring from her skin.

Their sounds had been many as they'd made love and the cage had nearly fallen apart, a wild clatter of clanking iron rising from within, sounds heard not by any general populace since the town office was closed by that time, but heard by Pierrette, standing behind the convenience store where she worked and smoking a cigarette, she and her unborn child smoking a cigarette, the child's taste for nicotine an eager and excitable one which Pierrette thought it unfair to deny. When the clatter of destruction from the barn had sorted itself down to a rhythmic metal on metal clink, she had smiled and gone inside.

6

They had been staff for a long time, a tiny team, more like sister and brother although Pearson wasn't sure about that since he'd had neither, no formal declarations of this or that needed—certainly not love—yet everything laid out and clear.

At noon on most days they would share leftovers that one or the other had brought from home. After lunch, with the door locked and the door and window shades pulled, they would each lie on one of the couches in front of the counter, a nap following of twenty-five minutes, no real sleep but a skirting of that funny fringe where thought does its work, Pearson's thoughts usually sexual and getting him hard, a knuckle nooner always unrequited though he'd half-dreamed one time that he'd told her, "If you were a referendum I'd vote for you twice. If you were a tax I'd pay you more than once," not surprised at all over the way in which office talk just never worked outside the office.

Liselle seemed to nap, too, though sometimes she would lie there with a magazine from home, hardly ever reading it, or a book. As she told him once, at night she would lie in bed with a pillow between her legs and a book in her arms. You couldn't be faulted, see, she'd said ("By whom?" he'd asked her once) if you fell asleep while actually doing something. He'd thought of all those bedtime readers out there slipping painlessly from guilt to somnolence and decided it was sweet that Liselle, boss or not, could be as silly as anybody.

"By whom?" he'd asked, a generic wonder that had wounded her. He'd only intended to deny the existence of some snooze cop peeking in windows to excoriate the lack of poetry or great recipes falling from your pen, or why you weren't doing the laundry or sealing the driveway.

Yet she took it as his commentary on there having

been no one in her bed in seventeen years, a snappy, painful commentary, she said, intended to destroy all the good she'd done, she and Pierrette, and he responded that women just don't like to be called to account for anything.

Having surveyed the wreckage of where they had done it, and having taken that coy dollop of nostalgia like an antidote for the morning's butchery of the children, Pearson closed the doors of the barn and locked the locks.

Nostalgia, he knew, as antidote, rarely worked for long.

7

As Pearson walked in from the barn Liselle was standing by the door. He looked immediately down her arms, down to her hands, those big hands of the boss, soft but large, nails neatly done and polished, wanting, frankly, to see motion there, to see those arms coming up to encircle him, a hug at least for this if not for all those Friday mornings he'd felt a victim of, or just for all those times he'd watched her adjust her bra or shift her butt in her chair or stand shoeless at the counter talking to someone, one foot raised and brushing the back of her calf, Pearson nearing self-immolation as he day after day watched the intimate crotch scratchings of power.

Well—and Pierrette, too, that genial body gassed up to near explosive pressures or able to pee great trenches in the snow (which she tended to do if she didn't want to walk over to the town hall, the convenience store, as Pearson had joked one day, not having a modern convenience). On another day, she stood in the door to the bathroom and brushed her teeth, her blouse open, her foamy whining oppressive in the small office. Pierrette had been up to something and had finally gotten her mother to come over to the bathroom. Liselle listened, then said: "Okay. Let me see," as she'd scooped the one breast out of the bra. The pimple, which was all it was, was obvious and fiery near the nipple. Pierrette was nearly hysterical. She spat flecks of toothpaste foam on Liselle's blouse until Liselle finally said: "It's not a lump. It's not what they mean."

"They were from Quilli," Pearson said, sitting down at his desk and looking over the stack of *Actuals* he'd placed there the day before. "I watched the one girl die. She could move, but the car was so tight in the tunnel she couldn't get out. Her arm was gone. Has anyone been asking about the accident?"

The first book, a bound volume two feet square, had no title on the outside, but on the first leaf had been written: *Lists and Actuals—St. Antoine de Plupart, Maine.* Subsequently, he found it to be only one of many, the books of the town, not only as in "keeping the books" or, as Liselle had told him one time, "They're supposed to do another audit of the books one of these days, the State, Pearson, bunch of fat-lidded boys and girls from away"—not only assessments and surveys, births, deaths, the laws, the actual laws of the town as determined by ordinance and adjudication over the decades, or accounts, billed and payable, billed and unpaid and thus: foreclosed, sadness in a column of figures. Not only those predictable things but other things as well, other figures: fuel oil, tar paper, lumber, twelve pounds of ointment(!) paid in full with no date on it, though he was in the 1920s at the time, and even some squiggles of fun: a side of beef, six hundred pounds of ice delivered one July, bills to the wheelwright that later turned into bills to Firestone down in Quilli, a good number of medical bills, too, somewhat puzzling since the town had never been in the practice of paying people's medical bills, except for a big bill in 1956 for Salk vaccine, a good gesture that, a responsible, civic gesture.

Yet it was in the margins that things took such a fascinating detour, a fine handwriting so small as to be difficult to read, except so neat—fingers from a school of high penmanship—that it was no problem, like a mist-filled conversation with the town and its events, other Liselles and even others of himself, town fathers, town mothers, flanksters, midpersons, dolts, and independents and those who knock on doorless buildings, all getting or receiving a small revenge in the record. Truth, he thought, will out—a can of fuel oil blew up (1933) in the mayor's face, mostly because he was divorcing his wife for her infidelities, throwing her right out onto the street on a really peppy winter day, beautiful with gauntlet clouds and crunchy, half-frozen puddles under a bright sun. So she sat, forty-three and feeling much the failure, a little singed, and then that account simply ended. Perhaps the day had ended and the clerk forgot to pick up the story again. Halfway down that page another entry began: "Children unruly. They will be shown. Seems to be about once a year now." Unruly only once a year? That was cryptic, something more than mischief but, again, there was no continuity in the account. Another one (1876) began: "We billed egs for St. A de P's common dole, increesed now by one with Sally's drop." Like that. The narratives increased in length and detail the farther back Pearson went, but still maddeningly tending to stop of a sudden and not resume.

8

"There is no horror in history," Liselle said, so softly and with so slightly a tilt to her head, nothing mischievous, she might have said, "Pearson, would you rub your tongue right here between my legs, please?" so controlling for him was her every notion.

Now and then he read to her the notes on those lives, those marginal lives, such a coldest of commentaries. She seemed irritated when he did it, and he thought they might just sound boring taken off the page, pulled away from the busy context of town business: accruals and abatements, easements, liens. That government is best which governs least. He, at least, was trying. Sometimes he wished Liselle bodiless, a mere essence of command.

"So her, how was it?, 'issue'? trailed her for two days

as she wandered naked in town? There isn't a cop who hasn't had a few of those. As I hear it, she must have tried aborting herself and ripped out her uterus. I don't *want* to know that about my cousins, darling."

"Life was mean," he said. "Pretty bleak."

"Especially if you sat on a pitchfork."

"She used a fireplace poker. It's interesting, though, because it's spelled p-u-k-e-r. Actually the whole sentence is—'Suspicion of a grate puker. Nothing to do.'"

"Apt enough."

9

Those lives on the margins chronicled little of any joy and Pearson wished someone over the decades had pointed that out to all those clerks.

Liselle was sitting on the edge of his desk, a cup of Pierrette's coffee in her hand. A scent was coming off Liselle that Pearson liked, a sniff of eros and fresh-ground Colombian beans. He noticed a small break in the stitching on her skirt and pointed it out to her. She stood then and twisted her skirt around so that the seam was in front, raising it well up onto her thighs before giving a quick sniff, or it might have been a grunt, he decided, and dropping it down, that thigh in

Pearson's face a place where he could have put his head and had a fine sleep, soft and old-fashioned, commodious, a lark and put that one in the margins.

More of those intemperate etchings came at him, pictures taken during an off decade, the ones that made his ankles itch or his heart seem to stop. A state legislator was married over at the tavern, his bride a sweetie of sixty-seven while he was barely twenty, obviously more popular than smart since she'd convinced him anyway that she was with child. Hungrily, Pearson scanned the margins for some word how that all turned out but he never found it.

Another day, a morning, he'd been staring at Liselle's back for the longest time, a good lot of it revealed in the sleeveless, low-cut summer dress she was wearing, her skin as always a blanket he could have pulled around himself, her skin warm and smooth as a fine ivory paint, the kind never on sale, a number of moles dotting around, friendly landmarks of an undangerous sort, though, no divots needing to come out of there by a surgeon looking for experience— when the itching had hit his ankles again, that achillean dermatitis of love. Crazy, he knew, telling himself it wasn't love of any sort, just a normal desire to please, all of it playful. Really, though, she wasn't his type and that was clear. He could be the boss's whore, if need be; he could be anything she wanted. But this love, clearly—*clearly*—could be taken care of with a little cortisone cream. Unlike, he thought for a moment, the reattachment of a teenager's head (or arm!)—that could only be done by God. Pearson sighed then: God. What a prankster.

If this be madness, he thought, there's failure in it.

That day, at noon, after only ten minutes on the couch, he'd gotten up, a chill of restlessness scooting through him. Liselle looked asleep on the couch near the window. He looked over at one of the big books open on his desk, forgetting which time period it covered and, after taking another look over toward Liselle—her feet were dirty and her hands were resting atop one another right over her groin—sat down, this thought from his snoozing state still there, still amenable to some shaping by his fountain pen and, finally, conscious of himself as pulling down a mantle or picking up a gauntlet thrown down again and again by time's own forgotten scribes, he wrote.

It was tiny. It was neat enough, a printing, though, his cursive not a thing you'd want sitting there in some state archive long after St. A de P was municipal mist, his first effort, he thought, too sweeping, too opinionated in a context that wanted a quotidian recounting of bread names and what was panty hose anyway? He wrote: *There are more diseases to be feared than ever before, and to be feared personally as dreaded possibilities.* Not what he meant, not at all. Some diseases could rip your arms from your body and he hadn't said that.

Still, suitably grim, a fit heritage, yet a hint of chattiness. A coldness was in the pit of his stomach, the chill of victory, of things that matter. He looked up from his desk and saw Liselle staring at him. She was sitting on the couch, but all he could see was her head, looking detached as though it were sitting there all alone on the counter. She looked sleepy and for a moment he didn't move, didn't smile. Their eyes met restfully without the barrier of word or expression. In a moment she'd get up and go to the bathroom and he'd go to the front and raise the shades on the windows and door and turn the black and pink CLOSED sign to OPEN. Sometimes there would be someone waiting there right at one o'clock and Pearson would let them in with a lot of bustle and merry talk so that they couldn't hear Liselle's sounds in the bathroom. The walls were damn thin.

10

Going back into the earlier volumes, he'd begun making his presence known, having discerned early on the one and only one rule: no scratch-outs, no erasures, no false starts. Incompleteness was, obviously and repetitively, all right. If the inner pages, the centers, were the precise domain of the auditors, the margins belonged to the people, and if the people didn't have to have conclusions, didn't have to have a point, they *had* to have the voice, the start, the unhesitating urge to go on record.

The effect on Pearson was profound and scary. By adding his own facts to the earlier facts, he was becoming part of everything. For someone forever a nonnative and a good fifteen years away from even being "from" St. Antoine de Plupart, he was now involved in things even the oldest families knew nothing about. *All living creatures can understand, yet less than one percent can offer insight as exchange.*

Hortatory, clever yet vacuous. He'd wanted to write

about the girl with the bleeding ears and that had come out. Fine. If he wasn't ready, he wasn't ready.

Liselle was on the floor in front of his desk, a large filing slew of water bills in front of her. She was on her knees and sitting back on her haunches. Now and again she would lean forward to this or that pile of paper slips, her desk-bound buttocks compressed, that day, in a tight skirt. Pearson thought of inserting a pencil somewhere back there, something he could sniff from time to time when the press of business seemed to take the humanity right out of him. When she leaned back, the skirt seemed coyly indifferent to where it stopped on her thighs. Pearson wondered if Liselle knew what she was doing to him.

11

Later, Liselle was sitting on the counter facing him, a cup of very old and very strong coffee in her hands.

"What do you have there?" she asked.

"It's a very delicate—or indelicate—account," he said. "But then, most of them are."

"Who was it?"

"A family. There aren't usually any names given. A

G. K. WUORI

man, a woman, I think three children. In a short sentence bad habits are mentioned and then the loss of a job at the mill—so this was a good while ago. They became hungry. That's all that's said, but you get the feeling there was a good lot of desperation. The man brought his wife to the tavern one day to try to sell her for either money or food. No one, however, was buying because she was supposedly part Mieuq Macque and the feeling was that you shouldn't have to pay for that. The same thing happened with his two daughters and even his son. There's mention of a dilemma here, people wanting to help but not able to violate their canon about the Indians, and the man not able to accept charity.

"At one point, it's said his cheeks were so gaunt you could see the shape of his upper teeth. Well, he announced to one and all at the tavern one night he'd give his testicles for a bag of flour. You can guess the rest. By spring, he was much the lesser having spent the greater part of his groin, four toes, both his ears, and the tip of his tongue (this latter involving a living fish). The oddest thing was not that nobody would help the family—although comments suggest they were disgusting, I think smelly, to be around—but that the first account that lays all of this out begins with: *A most resourceful man is among us, his love of wretched kin a trusted, treasured thing.*

"Pearson?"

"Yes?"

"How *are* you?" Liselle's legs were crossed at the ankles and for a moment Pearson saw himself leaping over his desk, his arm straight out like a jouster's pike, his hand diving into that bowel of shadow and, buttocks empalmed, hoisting Liselle overhead, both of them forgetting the dropped ceiling, her head pushing a panel upward at the same time that Pearson felt the entirety of his shoulder dislocating.

12

Love kept getting in the way of the butchery—four kids and he was trying to *understand* it? Was faith clashing with reason here?—which was, he thought, the way it had always been, his mind a poet intervening with its playful romps well before he actually had to *do* anything—not a good poet, though. Not well read, since he couldn't remember when he'd last read a poem, or anything else that didn't tell him how to do something; still, the poet in the closet, the coat pocket, the poet of hurts and envious causes, lamentations and beery toasts, source of personal rumors, transgressions.

Yes, he'd dicked and rumped his way through many a private moment, Liselle especially the wan confessor to his libido; no, to his spirit, the adventurer, the one here playing games of loss and chance with the delicate tale of a town's life. He wrote: *Each day, three thousand, seven hundred and seven gallons of human sperm are ejaculated.*

In St. Antoine de Plupart? God, he chuckled, a bunch of active little buggers. Worse, he thought that maybe he was enlarging his scope, going worldwide, and he wondered what that was all about. Making comments on the world scene was like spitting into the waterfall at Grand Falls. Every drop counts, yet none for very much.

Was it a ploy to win Liselle's hand? Even there, he couldn't remember ever having had a ploy before. Besides, that hand was not in the marketplace to be won or lost, that hand burned long ago in becoming a single parent with the help of her single husband who'd left leaving things quite singular. Liselle had few good things to say about men, and while he'd never felt himself to be any defender of the gender, he did think her experience a little limited. *The average American used to be familiar with five states and six towns. Today, those figures are, respectively, twelve and thirty.*

He'd written that on one of the margins of 1929, a year that couldn't have meant much to St. A de P. So how did he get from "the average American" to Liselle's nipple, to a grand love of sexual beneficence, trust, companionship, heartache, the real truth that beyond a few tears the loss of some careless kids meant nothing in a world where savagery was measured in pounds and counts and not degree of moral lapse? Pearson was embarrassed to admit even to himself that Liselle's nipple was a poetic ploy—fine enough even with the fine hairs (she'd told him about those)—but he really wanted to take on—to date? to take out?—one of her big toes, something public from that charming lady to be shown the world as his own. The removal of body parts, after all, was quite a tradition in the area.

"I'm all right," he finally said. "But here, let me read you this. It's scattered all over but I've put paper clips on the pages and I think I can keep it straight."

• • •

13

What was revealed in Pearson's own handwriting (as he read it to Liselle) was his attempt to hold both love and savagery in his mind at the same time. He wanted a picture—youth is beauty; beauty is youth—to counter the encroaching monster of car wrecks and headless, armless youths that was chewing at his brain like some untrained virus. He knew he would fail. It was the fate of legacies. But fantasy was the only thing left. All else was madness.

Pearson read: "We pulled the huge oak tub from our own landfill of historical legacy, our litterpot of legislative junk. It was a good five feet across and not at all old. I remembered the dePlupartFest where it had been a dunking tank, Liselle among the more memorable dunkees, wrapped in tissue and crepe paper commemorating some mythical French empress, the crepe paper even bleeding through her swimming suit and leaving her a striped and speckled and slightly diseased-looking mayor for days afterward.

"The tub, that night, we balanced on a wheelbarrow and slowly rolled it through the barn doors and out into the yard, the center of the yard between the

76

town hall and the town barn, well within reach of the hose I brought up from the basement.

"Pierrette's house was comfort taken to an extreme. A spare sixteen feet square, it was yet gabled and gingerbreaded, Victorian mostly, the inside carpeted and hardwooded and wainscoted and curtained, all patinaed and richly dark, even an old grandfather clock ticking its way into the gloom and scratching the shadows. The place was a steal from the woman in the nursing home at Quilli—the one run by certain nuns—and if all worked out it looked as though Pierrette would be a homeowner by the time she was twenty.

"We stood, our twosome, bent on example, outside in the dark. It was past ten and the house was unlit, the temperature twelve below zero. Liselle had a good idea that Pierrette was in bed, probably drunk from beer she'd sold herself at work. The door was unlocked, as Liselle knew it would be, and we went inside.

"We let Pierrette keep her nightgown on until we had the front door open, then Liselle bent down and grabbed the hem and whipped the gown off of her before she could react. The girl was thus naked. Wrong.

She was nude. Naked was unctuous and sinful. Nude was quiet, demure—royalty awaiting the majesty of wisdom. Holding the girl by the arms—both for security as well as her walk not being steady at all—we stepped outside.

"Pierrette pressed her head against her mother's chest as we walked the back yards to the town hall and the tub. Every few steps she would look up to Liselle and nod her head, whispering something once and then we stopped while Pierrette squatted down to pee. Apologetically, and with great difficulty, she tried to say it was all the baby or the beer, but by then Liselle and I were helping her into the tub, Pierrette so cold she didn't think anything could be colder, her nipples gumdrops of pucker, the baby a protected ball of heat in her abdomen.

"Still, she could only smile as her foot broke the thin film of ice on the water, the smile shy, slight, not visibly showing its route all the way up from her ankles, funny things happening all over the place with nerve and muscle, farewell spasms and good-bye jerks, defections and remembrances slowly shutting down as she slid further into the tub."

• • •

14

Pearson finished his account by saying they had used the town tractor with its winch to raise the block of ice up into the barn loft where it sat upright in the loft opening, the two doors swinging open and closed from time to time, the girl in there—and here Pearson paused, these final words needing to be important ones—a jewel against the dark inner barn, a diadem, a peach in a crystal prison, a tribute to something lost and foolish in youth everywhere, the child and her child deep within that frozen fog, a gentle smile on Pierrette's face, her eyes, amazingly, still open. In the morning some sharp, fresh sun would sparkle its way through the trees or the gaps and shrunken crevices of the cedar boards, a temporary painting of light and glitter, the children of St. Antoine de Plupart held up for all to see as in this place for beauty and the solace of awe, not mere fodder for the roads, compost for the ditches.

15

Pearson likened his work to things done in a minor fever, an inflammation of instincts, a thought that for his age control was a vicious myth and that it was time to lust openly for Liselle. Let her take charge, if she must do that. Command was never more than obedience, and he could bury her with a hard-driving, muscular subservience, covering her body with love poems written on sticky notes, cowering, groveling before her with his maleness wrapped in paper-clip chains. He could dance on the desk or take all the complaints that came through the door, clean the woodstove or sweep the door mud three, eight, twelve times a day.

She hated him and he knew that, hated their intimacy, their forced sharing of the ignorance of every jerk who walked through the door, hated his smells and his tributes and his cleverness and his helpfulness and even hated it when his back was out and he had to mince around like an old lady trying to tap dance in hunting boots—hated, above all, having given in to herself the one time, having trashed his dick in the old cage, Pearson regretful at not being some delighted stranger, a seller of municipal novelties politely disappearing into new territories and never setting foot in St. A de P again.

The auditors, for as far back as Pearson had ever bothered to read the reports, had never failed to comment on the marginal notes in all the books, informal letters praising the historical intent, suggesting, naturally, better devices, things formal yet more salutary, more room for detail in other vehicles, more room for the sort of secrets the fiscal mercenaries didn't need to see. Pearson smiled when he thought of those comments, smiled as he imagined the reluctant delight upon being assigned to do the books here, the wonder of those shabby people and their bawdy deeds. Pearson thought, Yeah, well, take that, creeps, and that and that, as he noticed a long streak of mud on the back of Liselle's leg, and kept on writing, writing slowly because he was trying a script so small he himself could barely make it out, a flush of tiny triumphs pinking up his cheeks as he moved his head back as far as he could while remaining at his desk and decided, yes, it was clear, clear and neat, tiny indeed yet legible, somewhere off to the left of three lines detailing expenditures for a small memorial to the dead kids, a gift from St. A de P to Quillifarkeag: *I love you, Liselle.*

Quitno Blêd's favorite meal was fried liver and sauerkraut, the kraut rich with brown sugar and caraway seed. Occasionally, he would bring a woman to his house and he would cook his favorite meal. It was, they said, a small price to pay for going out with a man like Quitno Blêd.

Quitno was an actual hero and Quilli gave him anything he wanted. It gave him food—he liked boiled heart, too, and boiled cabbage, and a coffee so strong that Don's Grocery had to import it from Burma. Some skeptics raised questions about that, about whether coffee was even grown in Burma (there had been a rumor that Burma was in North Dakota, a frequent rival to northern Maine in claiming the coldest days of the year), but the answer was always: "It's for Quitno Blêd."

End of discussion.

Quilli gave Quitno Blêd its women, too, a discrete arrangement and, of course, not all of them. His tastes were passionate for the unbathed sort, the undeodorized. In a hardworking town like Quilli this was not a major accommodation, nor was it hard for anyone to understand—not even the husbands of a few of those women. It was a sacrifice, the usual response to which was "But what the hell. It's for Quitno."

His heroism—this unrepayable debt—began at McDonald's late on a Friday morning.

At the time, Quitno was unemployed and sleeping in the cabs of construction vehicles. He had a little money, but no hope. It was a dark time. As one woman put it, "I hate to see a big man down. It's like watching Barney die."

Quitno *was* big. "Six and a half feet," he would say, "from there up to here, and I weigh about as much as the front porch on a small house."

Hungry, he'd gone into McDonald's for a coffee and the double quarter-pound cheeseburger that had become his favorite food since the company introduced it.

He noticed the strain on the clerk's face as she gave him his food. He even said, "The Metamucil not working today, mother?"—a friendly jibe to the woman who he thought must be in her eighties at least.

TURNING AROUND, THOUGH, WITH the burger and coffee in his hands, Quitno saw the children. There were—maybe—twenty of them, all very young.

They were quiet, too. Quitno thought that unusual. Children were never quiet in McDonald's.

Then he saw the woman. She must be with the children, Quitno decided, because they all stood near her. She, however, was on her back, barely conscious, and lying across two tables.

Quitno saw that she was wearing big furry ankle boots with the toes cut out, something his daughter had told him was the latest northern fashion.

Finally—this all happened very fast, of course— he noticed two more things.

First, it looked as though the woman's lower jaw had been punched up into the roof of her mouth.

Second, the injured woman, barely conscious, motionless across the two tables, was Quitno's daughter.

"She's a day-care worker," he'd said to someone just that morning. "How is she?" had been the final question.

He'd said at the time she was just fine.

Quitno thought the answers to most questions were temporary, and what he was looking at just then seemed to confirm it in a crazy way.

CLOSEST TO QUITNO IN the whole group was the skinny man with what Quitno later said were "straggly eyes." Unshaven and clearly no one anyone knew, he held a rifle in one hand and a grenade in the other, the pin of the grenade resting on the palm of Quitno's daughter's open hand. She had struggled, he saw. She had lost.

The children were up a creek. He could see that.

He wanted to run out of there: a natural instinct. Sweet reason said this was not his affair. A dramatic something ought to occur at a later time, something he had planned for. More or less—and thoughts occur so quickly in such cases it is always less—he just didn't think he was ready for injury or death. It was Friday morning after all.

But there were the children—that took a microsecond. There was his daughter—even less time.

. . .

QUITNO BLÊD TOOK TWO steps and poured his coffee over the skinny man's head. McDonald's made really hot coffee and Quitno was glad of it. Courage, however, can't function without luck and Quitno was pulling hard on both. After dropping the empty coffee cup he reached down and grabbed the grenade out of the man's hand, and with all of the dramatic strength that a big man can muster he sidearmed it right through a plate glass window and into the garbage Dumpster that was thirty feet across the parking lot. He had not, of course, aimed for the Dumpster. That had been luck.

As was reported by witnesses, the skinny man hadn't exactly lapsed into a stupor at this point, and the sound of the grenade exploding—truly, a real one—in the Dumpster muffled the sound of the skinny man's rifle going off as he raised it upward in his hand.

The bullet made a small crease on Quitno's forehead after taking off a good half of his nose. That crease would heal without a scar and the outside part of Quitno's nose would be rebuilt with skin and cartilage from his feet. He said there wasn't a lot of pain after the repairs, but it was still like going through life thinking it was time to wash your socks. Later he would tell people the injury lay behind his need for smelly women and strong food. Sometimes, joking, he would say he needed strong women and smelly food. Quitno didn't joke very often.

WHEN THE POLICE CAME the children were removed from the scene. The Dumpster was on fire, but it was containing the fire just as it had contained the grenade.

Quitno was sitting near his daughter, encouraged that she was beginning to move and starting to groan. With one hand he was mushing the double-burger cheeseburger against his wounded nose. With his other hand he was holding the skinny man by the neck and keeping him on his knees. Even the old woman behind the counter said she could hear the man's top vertebrae cracking from time to time. A few years later the skinny man was on a television show focusing on what it was like being a paraplegic in prison.

The police, as is their duty, politely suggested that Quitno Blêd had been foolish.

The town said Quitno Blêd was magnificent.

McDonald's gave him a Certificate for Life for Free

Food. He appreciated that but rarely used it. His daughter, speaking awkwardly through her wired jaw shortly after the incident, said her father, with only half a nose, had become so hooked on garlic that she felt like she was in an Italian restaurant whenever she visited him.

Not used to dealing with the media, she later apologized for her insensitivity to ethnic issues.

Law

CRIME

Ｉt is from common cloth that nobility is often cut, though sometimes that cloth can seem a mere hankie, a dishrag. Even punishment can enlighten, though sometimes that light can be so bright it disappears. At one time, St. Antoine de Plupart gave Belknap Bleu lots of credit. Then it closed her account.

Belknap Bleu, someone said, was as low as a bug.

The town clerk in a mean town like St. A de P is as much the town mother as she is the chief business officer, at least when she's Belknap Bleu or at least before she got herself indicted. It was a shame, since Belknap Bleu had replaced a man who'd fallen in love with the mayor and she probably could have had the job forever.

Town Hall is adjacent to the town barn, which houses the town truck, so it's a place for some of the boys to hang out, and certainly Belknap Bleu was worth hanging out for.

She had been a model at one time. She had breasts and a butt and a quality of leg that commanded respect from men whose wives had modest careers and shapes akin to plastic juice bottles. She had been in a Kmart circular for plus sizes, and she had sold cars on television for Jolly John down in southern Maine. She knew what it took to do those things, she said. She knew what it took to do a lot of things.

Belknap Bleu had poise, however, which iced everything in. A tilt of her head could be like an earthquake. A quick glance at her empty coffee cup could send someone running to the diner. Although she was faithful to her husband, Youthven—her poise once again—she knew the loneliness of the recently uncompanioned and didn't mind providing a seemly fantasy to some of the men who needed only that until a better future came along.

As CLERK, BELKNAP BLEU was entrusted with the town funds. Gas could be had at the town pump for cost, as could a load of gravel or a tank full of heating oil (the paper would later joke that the town garage must have been tropical, burning twenty-seven thousand gallons of oil in a winter). General Assistance, too, never an easily accountable fund, got many a family through to payday with cash for groceries.

Mostly, Belknap Bleu returned to the citizens that which was theirs. Then, as it happened, she returned to Belknap Bleu that which was theirs: $5 per tax payment to her purse.

They nailed her for $375.

"CORRUPTION!" WAS THE SMALL cry in the tiny town of St. A de P.

"It was like," someone said, "she gave me money for breakfast and then stole my lunch."

On the judicial level, "violation of a public trust" reverberated with all the solemnity of bad news coming from a young doctor.

On the state level, she was one of three town clerks in Maine cited for similar offenses that year.

On the national level, she was mentioned (by town, not her name) in a law review.

AT HER ARRAIGNMENT, ADMISSION, and sentencing—all held at the same time, no one wanting to make *too* big a thing of things—she lost her job, was fined $500 and told to make restitution of the $375 they could account for, and was told to do community service. This latter was hard, since in a community like St. A de P the town clerk provided about all the service anyone needed and Belknap Bleu wasn't that anymore.

Back home, she was now jobless and had to sell Youthven's La-Z-Boy to help with the restitution. As a joke, Youthven made her a little collar out of a strip of sheet metal. He stamped COMMUNITY SERVICE on it and put it around her neck with a couple of pop rivets.

It was an evening's joke, but when Youthven said, "Let me get the tin snips. I'll cut it off," Belknap said, "No. I think not."

The next day, Belknap went out and cleaned up St. A de P's only park, a one-acre plot with one old bench and a small statue of St. Antoine de Plupart. She worked in shorts and a T-shirt that turned sweaty fast and old sandals that flopped and slapped as she walked the bagged trash out to the transfer station on the edge of town.

On another day, she got a bucket of paint and redid the stripes down the center of Main Street. It was not highway paint, but then the street was not a highway.

She got white paint on her feet and knees, and the way she squatted onto each stripe it looked like she was peeing her way down the street.

Some of the women in town thought there was a little too much spectacle in her service. Others said a lot of pride was emerging from her guilt.

She cleaned the culverts under the driveways next, some of which were big enough to crawl through, and she did that wearing an old bikini she'd bought in 1971.

People began to worry because she was getting a lot of cuts on her body. Youthven said he was rubbing her down with Bag Balm every night. He said you just don't know how sorry she is.

During the first snowfall the plow truck didn't even make it out of the barn: a cracked piston. Belknap Bleu did the streets by hand. It took her two days and was a hot job. She'd start with the parka and jeans on and end up wearing only boots and long underwear.

THIS WAS ALL A spirited thing and everyone knew it. Eventually, an amount of traffic made its way to the town. Someone had heard from someone who'd heard: they had her collared and shackled, even branded.

When Youthven made the shackles for her, the town said it was over and that she could stop. Youthven Bleu responded to that, the next spring, by painting Belknap red—the color of guilt. That alleviated concerns about the way she was increasingly doing town work naked, wearing only the sheet-metal collar and the ankle chains, but things slid back up to a fever pitch when the small signs appeared that said SUNDAY—A PUBLIC BRANDING.

Youthven did that, too, though the only public who showed up was a family from Quilli looking for someone who'd advertised a litter of beagle pups for sale. The mother in the family told her husband, "First tattoos, then piercing—now this? Here? Can you imagine what's going on in New York?"

Which missed the point, since what was going on in St. A de P was far more advanced than almost anything going on anywhere. Youthven said that, not testimony so much as a family story told with pride. Full justice required some scheming, a little sleight of hand.

Main Street needed repaving, a job Belknap Bleu couldn't do. A county crew was brought in, the street stripped and dug up, a new gravel base put down.

Early one morning—the level finisher having been

brought to town the night before—Belknap Bleu and her husband dug a small trench in the center of Main Street.

"There is much here of the Roman," she told Youthven, "of the Romanesque. When you betray someone, you become a part of them. I am now my town."

Youthven covered her up. Dawn was barely breaking and the first of the asphalt trucks had not yet arrived in town. They would, though, or as Youthven often said, sitting on the La-Z-Boy that someone had mysteriously returned, "They did."

REVENGE

Johnny had fingernails—truly, not nubby, chewed things but products of pride in his appearance—yet they were not good enough. The two men had taped his one hand to the cooler door handle with damned tough tape, taped it round and round and round, and he couldn't even make a nick or slice in it with the nails on his free hand. He'd even walked the door around until it was almost closed so he could reach in and grab a thing of yogurt and rip the lid off—the stuff spilling down his leg as it plopped to the floor—and slice at the tape with the plastic lid but it did no good.

Time was going on and they had his wife.

Without that, he would have been calmer. He would not have wasted time hefting the door to see if he could get it off its stainless steel hinges.

He wouldn't have taken those few moments to assess the bottles of oil behind him on the shelf to see if he could grab one and smash the glass of the door. That, too, wouldn't have done any good since the bottles were plastic. It was just the idea that some kind of trashing might indicate progress toward getting out of this.

They were still out there. One of them was doing something to his, Johnny's, car, while the other was gassing up their own. Janice was out there, too, and looking in at him, her wrists taped together, one end of a short piece of rope tied around her arm just above the elbow, while the other end was looped and tied into the rear door handle.

In the beginning, he had looked closely at the two men. No masks. No panty hose pulled down to the neck. Two men as visible as anybody coming in for chips and soda or a sub and a six-pack of beer. Clean-shaven, both of them easily in their forties, maybe fifties, one of them over six foot with red hair—that bothered Johnny because Janice had red hair—and the other up in the high fives and fat, wearing khaki pants and a wide, black belt that cradled his pot, a stiff-legged walker with 'roids and workman's hands, liver spots, too, and mostly gray hair.

Then Janice had come out of the bathroom and had seen the gun and the two men. She had seen them and been calm, acting poised but irritated the way women sometimes do in a crisis while men stand around with their thumbs up their butts plotting later revenge. Johnny had been standing there, his hands out but not quite elevated—no one had said, "Hands up, Buster!"—palms out, willing to go through all of this and give the men everything they wanted if only they didn't go crazy with the gun. He wondered why they had to bring the gun into it along with the loose bowels and the adrenaline burp when it all could have been so easy without it. After all, Quilli had only one night-shift cop and no dispatcher. Didn't they know? Everyone knew that.

Janice, though, went right to the register and opened it. She put all the bills and change into a bag, even the stash of bills and checks under the register tray. Unchoreographed, they had all moved then. Johnny raised his arms way up in the air and stepped toward the cooler. The man with the gun looked right at him and smiled, even though Johnny didn't want to see him at all, didn't want that face locked so tight in his brain that only a bullet would get it out.

The other man, the one with the pot and poached hands, walked over to Janice and shoved his hand right into the top of her dress, squeezing, Johnny thought, hard enough to bring an awful look to Janice's face.

All right, Johnny decided, so a free feel is part of this. You lose your livelihood and you lose—other things. We know this.

She dropped the bag when he did it, and when she went to pick it up the man rammed her hard in the hip with his knee and sent her sprawling behind the counter. Janice's dress flew up around her waist and Johnny could see she was embarrassed.

IN THOSE FEW MOMENTS Johnny felt successive waves of just about everything passing over him, including amazement as the man reached down and pulled off Jan's stockings and her shoes. Johnny continued to stand by the cooler. He wanted to shout "Just cooperate, Jan!" except that she was, or was trying to. Johnny felt as though he were being held in place by other forces—good sense, he hoped—the gun merely molded metal, his thoughts much more than that.

Finally, the gunman said, "Let's get this guy secured," and Jan stood up as her attacker moved away to get a roll of duct tape for Johnny's hands.

Let's get this guy secured? These were no leak-nosed dopers out for cash and wine. In fact, Johnny had already noticed that the gunman was wearing a class ring and had his neck shaved the way a hairstylist or good barber will do. Again, that thought bothered him since he thought he now had far too good a description of both of them than was healthy. On health, his feelings almost gave out: they still had Jan tied to the side of the car.

As the gunman, outside, tossed something from Johnny's car out back he looked in through the window of the store, and Johnny tried to look passive or cooperative or just generally not causing any trouble. The gunman pulled a pint bottle of liquor from his own car and came back inside. He walked to the paper goods shelf and ripped open a bag of plastic cups. He poured some into a cup and drank it, then poured some more that he started sipping as he walked back outside.

Janice looked right at Johnny and Johnny stood as straight as he could. He wanted to look strong and ready for her should something come up. He worked hard on the tape and he hoped she could see that, although if he worked too hard the freezer door would pop open, so he had to watch it. There might be some glare from the drive lights that could attract attention but he wanted to gauge that. Jan's eyes looked glazed, an odd look, something wicked in her fear. He continued working on the tape. There was movement there, progress, but not freedom. Not yet.

JAN HADN'T HAD TO come down from upstairs. She'd said she couldn't sleep, but that happened often and mostly she would read for a time, using the tiny reading flashlight so as not to disturb Johnny, even if it was a Saturday night when they stayed open until two or three and he wasn't even in bed yet.

But she'd come down, had gotten dressed and put on some makeup and hose and brought him a piece of pie from their kitchen and a glass of milk. She'd also put a piece of cheddar on the plate and they'd talked, a gentle and nowhere talk, a small laugh, a breathy sigh, not anything to add up to anything and all the more worthwhile for that.

Now Jan was out there. She had already put up with

ings you don't put up with in a normal day, had been handled and forced around in a way that, as Johnny saw it, meant that those two guys had given up their right to live.

They had given it up.

Johnny was startled by the thought, a heavy, bold thought, though it was not a hard thought in a place like Quilli, where the fine points of anything get smoothed out so quickly they often disappear.

Fine minds in courtrooms could decide what they wanted but, whatever this was, as Johnny lived it, it was just a people thing, the four of them, and something would be worked out. Even executioners can think things through.

BOTH OF THE MEN got in the car and Johnny looked down to his hand to see if the tape had really loosened up or if it felt that way because he'd managed to rip all the hairs out around his wrist. You cooperate and it does no good. You don't cooperate and suddenly you're someone's problem and they don't have much time. He heard the engine of the car start and he looked out to see Jan bending toward the driver's window. She was trying to talk, Johnny saw, trying very hard.

As the car began to move Johnny bent his head down to his wrist and began chewing on the tape, funny thoughts coming to mind like the way Jan had been suggesting they blacktop the drive and now she was out there on that gravel with no shoes on.

He was chewing furiously, certain that he'd heard Jan yell but not wanting to take even a moment to look up. The thing was, he thought, if you could get through the first thirty seconds of this you could make it, those first instants being the time when you had to plan something, try something, with nothing in your head functioning very well. That was your disadvantage because no matter how impulsive the event was, the intruder still knew what he wanted to do. His end was clear and all you had was time.

They were driving around the parking lot in a circle, going slowly with Jan tied to the car, speeding up for an instant, slowing, stopping hard—repeating that. Jan kept up. She held herself just inches from the car, strength, Johnny saw, still there, an abundant poise.

She lost her balance once. Her hip hit hard against the car as they came around the gas pumps. She went down on one knee and ended up sitting on the drive as he speeded up again, dragging her with her arms overhead but still working the situation, her legs pumping furiously until she finally managed to lurch to her feet.

Her dress was ripped and her mouth bleeding from where she'd bitten her tongue. She leaned forward to the window and shouted something at the driver. In a blind, backward punch, though, his fist came out and caught her on the nose, not enough to knock her out, but enough to bloody it and stagger her backward and off her feet again.

All Johnny saw was Jan losing her balance, her body going perpendicular to the car as they made the turn around the pumps. Her legs swung out over the island and knocked over the windshield wash and a rack of oil containers.

Jan, on her feet, limped badly as Johnny came through the door. His hands were red with blood from several bad cuts he'd chewed into the one wrist. He knew he didn't have much thought left inside at all, but his life seemed tool enough—a thing to use. No thoughts of bravery came to mind, nothing of courage or heroism. It was just a matter of tools, of craft.

For several years they'd kept a gun near the register until he'd finally decided he couldn't do business that way. Too many locals felt free enough to ring up their own sales if Johnny was busy. Temptation should never be communal, especially with old Quitno Blêd in town tempting the hero in everyone.

The gun was packed away. Although he tried to think if there was anything else around that he could use as a weapon he knew there was not. He had some garden tools toward the back but the executive out there had his own gun and all Johnny could do was test his will, which seemed considerable now and cruel as well.

The car was parallel to the porch as Johnny stepped outside. It was barely moving and both men had their heads turned sharply toward Jan, the executive with his arm in the passenger window, gun in hand and pointed forward. Fat boy, Johnny thought, the driver, looked like he was trying to pop Jan again.

Johnny did two things then where he might have surprised himself by being able to do even one. He walked up to the car, his eyes on the gun and nothing else. The man's hand was on the butt of the gun, and Johnny found his mind thinking, *That's good,* no finger on the trigger. Johnny put both hands on the gun and pulled so hard on it he spun himself around in a complete circle. He ended up still facing the car with only a second's worth of disorientation to get through.

He knew the next step was panic—theirs—and that if the driver floored the gas pedal he'd have one good shot from the gun (which had damn well better be loaded, he hoped—after all this) and if that didn't work, well, he just couldn't think of how bad, how awful it would be for Jan.

By the time he completed his disorienting spin the gun was in Johnny's right hand and his left was already wrapped into the executive's hair. Johnny forced the man's head back onto the headrest so that he could rest the barrel of the gun on the bridge of the executive's nose—the effect was noticeable—while still pointing it directly at the driver's head.

"I don't want you to step on the gas," Johnny said quietly. "None of us know what'll happen if you do. Maybe nothing. Maybe everything. Uncertainty's a bitch, we all know that."

"What do you want us to do?" the executive said. His words sounded packed in clay as they came out of his tightened throat.

"I don't know," Johnny said. "Shit, I'm pretty scared."

"Okay," the driver said. "My foot's off the gas. It's off the goddamn gas."

Hostaging doesn't work unless someone cares, Johnny thought. He didn't know if either of these guys cared about the other. He also didn't know if there might not be more weapons lying about. For a moment, he felt more vulnerable than when he'd been tied to the freezer with the smiling corporate type holding the gun on him. It was all in Johnny's hands now and it was quiet, yet he felt unprepared for leadership.

"It's off the gas, guy," the driver said again. He had his foot up on the hump, wiggled it almost cutely so that Johnny would see. Johnny looked at the foot and noticed he was wearing the kind of sneakers you can pump air into for a tight fit. Ruined, he thought, as he fired the gun into that foot.

THE NOISE WAS HORRIBLE, yet through it he could hear a scream from Jan.

Under Johnny's other hand, the executive's head was shaking, his body nearing a spasm. Johnny couldn't tell what kind of state the driver was in (awkwardly, the thought popped in, Footloose?, strange as could be). With his knee jammed onto the hump and with the steering wheel there the driver couldn't reach his foot, but he kept trying. He was noisy, too. He moaned a lot, cursed and cried, finally threw up all over the wheel and his lap and the dashboard.

Time to act, Johnny thought. If they had any more weapons or any presence of mind at all to try something they'd all just have to duke it out because he had to tend to Jan now. He released the executive to his tremors and walked around the rear of the car, grabbing a utility knife near the fallen oil rack as he did so.

JAN'S DRESS WAS IN shreds and she was standing mostly on one leg, the other bent slightly at the knee. Both legs were bloody. She looked up at him and Johnny thought, *You're such a peach* as she tried to bring a smile to that dirty and puffy face. Johnny noticed the contact lens sitting there on her cheek, looked like an edge of it had dried into a bit of blood, a fascinating bit of something, but he didn't think there was anybody he could ever tell it to. He picked it off with his fingernail and dropped it into his shirt pocket. He hoped it hadn't been scratched.

"I kept thinking of it, Johnny," she said.

"It's all right," he told her. He had the knife down to her wrists now, the tape all twisted up and tight and tough. A breast had come out of her bra and he brushed it with his ear as he bent close to try to find a spot to stick the knife in.

"Like when I'm raking or mowing," Jan went on, "or painting or doing anything long and repetitive and a song goes through my mind, just one or two lines which might be all I know of it, going over and over again except that now I can't even remember what it was."

The men had been looking at Jan's dishevelment and the breast and laughing when Johnny'd grabbed the gun and he thought, Sonofabitch, just making fun of someone like that. She had to stand there showing them her blood, more intimate than a striptease. It pissed Johnny off.

He understood how a cop might haul off and whack somebody he'd been chasing even though the person was finally subdued. A lot had gone out of him—Johnny—with that bullet into the guy's foot. Jesus, it's a mess in there. Blood and vomit and sneaker bits, a gun smell mixing with the moans and squirming going on in the car, all of it awful, and Jan still standing there humming and talking. "Can you believe that, Johnny? In my head I was joking all the time. I had my own death on my mind but I was going to laugh all the way and I don't suppose I took it serious enough, but, anyway, how'd all this happen, Johnny? What's going on here?"

JOHNNY'S ACTION HAD NOT been cathartic. A scruffy fizz still boiled within and the quiet evening of before refused to return. Worse, things seemed to be building up again. He even thought he was smiling—calmly and approvingly—when Jan, her hands finally free, reached in to the driver and patted his cheek, almost tenderly, then dug her nails in and dragged them from just under his ear to his mouth.

"I guess it's a shitty glory, though," she said, looking down at her hand and going "ugh" as she wiped it again and again on her torn dress.

Together they walked around to the other side of the car. Both of them concluded that the driver would be fine for a time, somewhat removed, change coming over him like a quality anesthetic.

"Why don't you get out of the car now," Johnny said to the executive. The man made no sound but his arm, not an aggressive arm, Johnny thought, flopped out of the door with his wallet in his hand. The wallet was open and Johnny could see the edges of some cash and some credit cards tucked in there. "I understand," Johnny said. "I really do. It just doesn't apply here, though. Not really, fella."

"We don't take American Express," Jan said from behind Johnny. An acceptable attempt at a laugh came out as she said it and Johnny smiled at her.

Johnny didn't think it fair that the driver should have to take the brunt of their trying to even all of this out. He brought Jan around and, after taking the wallet from the outstretched arm, brought that hand up onto Jan's breast.

"Johnny?"

"What it's all about, isn't it buddy?" Johnny said. "Something like that. Goddamn mean thing to do though, isn't it?" He pushed the arm away then and bent down to look at the man. "You do anything with that besides chew gum? Do you talk?"

"Whatever you want. This is all yours now."

Johnny stood up. "Well shit—sure. It's all me now. You make the mess, I clean it up."

"Take the wallet," the executive said. "I got cash, credit cards. I got I.D. in there and it's really me. Do whatever you want."

"Really you?" Johnny asked, quite loud. "Why in the hell would it be really you? Why would you do that?"

JOHNNY SHOT HIM IN the wrist then. He heard a hard gasp from inside, a strange breathing. Obviously, things had evened out now, the lines redrawn for a relationship.

The arm was still straight out. The door opened slowly as the man tried to keep the arm centered in the window opening. His hand was a mess, not bleeding all that much, but distorted from where the bones were broken.

"You would have killed her," Johnny said. Jan was holding the door open while the man sat sideways on the seat, his feet on the gravel. He had taken his arm by the wrist and was trying to press it into his stomach: painful, but protective.

Johnny thought: I have hurt them worse than they'd hurt Jan, but still the tension isn't draining. They probably didn't know she'd never bring him pie and cheese again and you had to think about that. That was a change and it was no damn good.

"We wouldn't have killed her," the man said. "My God—listen, we need some help here."

Don't sneak that goddamn tone of authority in here, thought Johnny.

"Are you listening to me?"

There was no reason why Johnny couldn't lose his mind in all of this—he hadn't been in a courtroom in at least twenty years yet already possible defenses were popping up—though at the time he was feeling much more complex than someone who just happened to have this simple thing to lose—there it goes—to be found again after some calm searching. I run a little shop here, is all, he thought, Route 161, Quillifarkeag, Maine, occasionally omitted on cheap maps. It's in my interest to be cheerful, to smile until my ears feel heavy. No one comes here to buy despondency or the rage of a merchant. I am tone deaf, yet the tone is up-beat. Gently do you lead the grumpy to the door and wish them a good day. Of course, it is not always what you want. These two here—a case of a case in point. Mean people and ransackers, brutalizers high on the Lord. Oh, hell.

"What's the other guy doing, Jan?" Johnny asked.

"He's not dancing," she said.

"Honey."

"I don't want it to end, Johnny."

"I know."

THE OLD GARAGE WITH its two bays was empty and had been that way ever since Don's Grocery had built its Auto Centre. Johnny had thrown some plastic on the floor to protect the cases of hard goods he occasionally stored there, but other than that it was unused and it was rare that Johnny even went out there.

He took Jan over to the old spring-loaded door and together they lifted it, both of them keeping an eye on the car, both of them hoping, in a way, to see it start to drive slowly off, to let this thing, through default or neglect, simply be over.

"Any idea how pissed off those two are right now?" Johnny said.

"Like me," Jan said quietly, the fact simply there and not necessarily being driven into any point.

Johnny reached over and touched her face where there was redness and some swelling. "I know," he said. "I wasn't forgetting you." He put his arm around her and held her for a moment, then stepped back and tried to smooth and fold the ripped pieces of dress over her breast.

"I guess I thought all I had to do was grab the gun, call the police, and make a pot of potato salad for tomorrow," Johnny said. "Little moments like this still get by me. What do you need?"

"Nothing. I feel stiff and getting stiffer. My hands hurt but I don't think anything's broken. I'm all right."

"I shot them, shot them both. Just like that. I wonder if I could do it again?"

"You did it once. That was fine. They're not going to go, are they?"

"No. I don't see how."

"They're pissed. You said so. They'd come back someday."

"Think so? I don't know. The one guy seems pretty smart, seems a guy who knows his beginnings and his endings."

"Careful, Johnny. Right now they could say the couple up at the store just went crazy and shot them.

I don't know if anyone would believe that but if you can start out off the hook it's harder for them to put you back on it."

"Any ideas? Find the night-shift cop?"

"Sure, but Johnny—"

If there was an old self to Jan, something of constancy and prediction that had vacated itself for a time, Johnny thought he saw it again. Maybe a furrow to the brow, pursing of lips—answers to practical problems. For a moment she seemed uninjured, unbludgeoned, the night not so bad after all.

"—I don't want to. Not yet."

NEITHER OF THEM PROTESTED as Johnny led them toward the grease pit. Johnny assumed they were thinking he was taking them inside to tend their wounds before the police came. "John, John, John," he sighed aloud, the executive saying, "Excuse me?" as Johnny brought him to the edge of the pit, surprising himself—This guy really has no idea what's coming, he thought—at how light a touch to the shoulders it took to push him in. He did notice a flash of residual instinct as the man wrenched himself around enough to avoid falling on the injured hand. Johnny thought he heard an ominous crack, though. Bones, he thought, bones, bones.

The other man was even easier, limping and trusting, weeping. Johnny was holding one of his arms with his hand and had his other arm across the man's shoulders. A strong smell of shit and sweat was coming off the man, a lot of iron in the blood, Johnny decided. They approached the pit and before the man even noticed anything amiss Johnny took a sharp turn and just let go.

There were cries as Johnny slid a plywood sheet over the hole. He thought of weighing it down with some cinder blocks in the garage but didn't. Those two boys weren't climbing anywhere.

Strange feelings were going at Johnny. Hard feelings, conciliation and lots of regret over things he thought were stupid, a sense that, pain for pain, things were about at a match, except for the living part. He couldn't get rid of the feeling that they'd given up any right to continue the process. No downward sloping of the high spirits of combat seemed able to change that, yet he couldn't pin down where he might be at in the agent business.

Certainly, he could not stand above them at the

edge of the pit and fire shots down into them. He couldn't do that. Nor could he give chase if they somehow managed to climb out, one of them standing on the other's back, maybe, pretty tough considering the injuries he knew about, the ones before the fall. But if they did, if they really did, he wouldn't care. Let them go wherever they might, tell whatever stories they wanted. Location, he thought, is all the truth you ever need, and he and Jan were here.

"Jan?"

She was standing behind the counter inside, one foot on a chair, putting an elastic bandage on an ankle.

"Did we kill them, Johnny?"

"Come here, Jan."

"What?"

"I want to look at you. Are you all right?"

"I'm all right."

IN THE MORNING HE went out back first thing to check on where he'd put the car. It was in an L where the garage attached to the house and store, parked and locked and looking normal, as though anyone who would need to would know whose car it was.

Johnny was pleased about the morning, one of those perfect fall sunrises that brought back the memory of other perfections, the sharpness of chill with the promise of warmth later on, the sky a bottle blue and no clouds anywhere.

HE WENT INTO THE garage expecting to find the plywood sheet thrown and the pit empty. The sheet was in place, causing him to look around quickly— someone waiting, two-by-four in hand. There wasn't even a sound.

He took an old furring strip and pushed it against the corner of the plywood. I anticipate a smell, he thought, and it's bad enough that I have to go out and clean your car. Foot blood, smelly foot blood and a lot of puke from your favorite foods.

"Morning, boys," he said. There was no response.

"Hello?" He leaned over and looked into the pit.

The executive was lying in a corner, one pant leg pulled up over his knee. Even in the dimness Johnny could see the swollen shin, the bone—no sliver here, looked like the whole lower bone—sticking out. He'd taken his shoe off and the foot was swollen, too, the tiny red dots of his painted toes gleaming a happiness certainly inappropriate for the moment. You should be careful of your toes if you think you might be in an accident. Sounds like something a mother would say.

He looked at the other man in the other corner who was looking up at him with tears running down his cheeks—or cheek. The nose was clearly broken, mashed really—he must have landed on his face, Johnny decided—the one cheekbone caved in, the skin raw. These two dogs been out in the sun too long. Still, he bet they both had children, probably grown children by now, some sort of assortment between the two of them who would have been stunned—stunned? decimated? traumatized?—or just upset to see their dads like this. It's just your tragic gore, you know, the thin air, the fetid smell, a touch of slime, of offal. Bones break under stress. "That's my thought, gentlemen," he said. "Maybe later we can all go down to Bud's and have a drink."

The only movement was in the workman's eyes as Jan and Johnny stood over the pit some days later. Johnny had brought a case of baking soda out and together they were emptying the boxes onto the men. "Hold your hand over your face," Johnny said softly to him. His eyes blinked but there was no other motion.

"I understand," Johnny said.

Earlier, he had opened the door to the other bay to let some fresh air in and Jan had suggested the baking soda for the smell. Even with the chill nights and cooling days the smell had been sour and growing. Both of the men were covered with the powder now, looking ghostly and the workman a trifle bizarre as that red-rimmed stare locked on to them through his dusted face. Johnny wondered if he was trying to see up under Jan's shorts.

He closed the door then and Jan waited while he took the case of empty boxes out to the Dumpster in back.

It was nearly noon and the morning had been busy with both of them working the register and Jan running out to pump gas. Technically, their two pumps were self-serve, but they offered the service whenever they could because a lot of the women felt comfortable with Jan and knew her anyway. The men just seemed to enjoy the service.

Jan was wearing sandals and shorts and a heavy sweater, her short, reddish hair shining in the high sun. Only a small red mark under her eye and the slightest limp remained of her encounter with the two men. The incident was done, however, for her. It had been an unfortunate thing, but you either let it scar and cripple or you didn't and much of that was just a function of what you thought about.

Johnny, though, had this idea that the two men in the pit had corporate origins, that the one with the silver-reddish hair and the tanning salon look was too distinguished to be some sort of ordinary stick-up guy, whatever that was, and Jan disagreed with that. Neither thought it was an important disagreement.

As they'd driven her around the parking lot she'd heard them talking in the midst of their laughter and great fun and she'd noticed that the corporate one had a lisp, nothing prissy but a hard garbling of certain sounds, enough, she thought, to keep you from going very far up anyone's ladder, let alone any corporate ladder. That was her point and Johnny just said, "Okay."

They were both disappointed that the two hadn't tried to escape, had felt fear change to a sense of burden by the way they just lay there, the pit, Johnny thought, not all *that* deep. After Sunday he'd even left the plywood sheet askew so they could see the opening and have some light to think and talk about things. Sunday, too, he and Jan had even talked about feeding them, but the conversation had been brief.

"Are you going to give them something to eat?" she asked.

"Are you serious?"

"Very—I mean in an abstract way."

"Oh. Well, no, I'm not going to feed them. Are you?"

"I couldn't do that. I don't even want to go in there, Johnny. Scares me just to think about it."

"Of course."

"I know."

So they hadn't, relying on escape instead, and now growing frustrated, even angered, because that didn't seem to be happening. Jesus, he thought, they don't even yell.

"Do you suppose we're letting them die?" she asked when Johnny finally came around from the Dumpster. Johnny hadn't been thinking at all at the time so her question caught him off guard.

"Who?"

"Johnny!"

"No—I mean, you just caught my mind out of gear. Uh—"

"I think we are," she said.

"They're free to go."

"Yes and no. They can but they can't."

"I know. So are we. We could take a trip. Just go and go for a few days."

"Why?"

"I'm bothered by being bothered," Johnny said. "Even annoyed."

"It's almost noon, Johnny. It'll be busy soon."

"Let's have lunch. I made some shrimp salad this morning."

"Johnny—I threw an apple down there earlier. I didn't mean to, but it hit the one guy on his head, near that bad cheek."

"And?"

"He looked at me. It landed in his lap but he didn't move. I'm still wondering if he ate it."

"Do you want to go see?"

"No."

"Good."

"But what if he did? What if he wanted the food, the strength? I felt bad when I gave it to him, like I was betraying us or something. Then I was pissed because he just sat there, like he doesn't care or—"

"Hush, Jan. It's all right."

"I don't know."

Johnny's arm was across her shoulder, his fingers on her neck and gently rubbing it. Jan told Johnny she was hungry and that they ought to eat before things got busy the way they usually did from noon until two. Then she said she had to go to the bathroom but stopped on the way in to pick up an old comb that was lying on the ground.

"Look Johnny," she said. "I bet it's theirs, or one of theirs. Older guys like that—they still carry combs, you know? What do we do with the damn comb?"

Johnny thought for a moment it was all hysteria, parts of an old Jan from a lot of years of marriage mixing with something new here. She was not—he could see this—sad, not even confused. Once, she even said, "It's, really, just a trash problem. I think so." There was a harder look to her eyes now and Johnny felt proud of her.

"Jan?"

"What, Johnny?"

"Everything's all right. It really is."

"Oh, I know that—damned all right, too. I have to kick me once in a while for my lack of faith in us, how we keep making it, you and I, day after day, problems booted in the butt that I couldn't even have imagined before, let alone resolved, but we do it, the two of us, and when it's all done I wonder what in the hell's going to happen next when I should be looking in a mirror and smiling like a crazy person. Sonofagun. Holy cow. Jan and Johnny—what a pair. Am I making any sense?"

"Dignity?"

"Is that what I'm talking about?"

"I am."

"Okay. Sure. You might say it has a certain ring to it. A little old-fashioned, maybe, but—here." She handed Johnny the comb and walked inside. He threw it in the trash can on the pump island.

BY SATURDAY THE TREAT and spectacle of early fall had passed and it was warm and rainy. Neither of them had been in the bay area since early in the week, although Johnny had closed the one overhead door on Thursday morning, concerned finally about what might start to creep in there rather than whether or not it was possible to get out. Before doing so he had stepped inside holding his nose, and pushed the plywood sheet back squarely over the pit. He saw it then and lamented that sometimes things just happen too late. Whatever you try there is a timing, often a split second between a deed and indifference, things done that might be noticed, or the hole in one by the solo golfer where there was so much more involved than a ball and a cup and a word of honor. My word, my honor, he thought, but only at the right time. Otherwise, it was nothing at all. He kicked the half-eaten apple core outside before closing the door, then picked it up and threw it hard toward the woods on the other side of the road.

Due to an unfortunate misspelling on his first shingle, Hubert Peterbuoy had what was commonly referred to as a "low practice."

"What," he was often asked (and later, always in a joking context), "is a low lawyer? Is that a redundancy?"

In Quilli there is no balloon so fat it can't be pricked by the thin pin of wit.

Lawyer Peterbuoy ignored the jests. He saw the law as being that part of wisdom that people could understand. Otherwise, he said, wisdom was like a big blob of pizza dough. It comforted. It was soft. It smelled good. Beyond that, any further use just gave you heartburn.

LAWYER PETERBUOY'S PRACTICE WAS limited to the defense of abusive men. This was the real reason, some said, he was called a "low lawyer." He could be eloquent in detailing how abuse arises, citing torts and crimes, the anguish of dead affection, the languishing and snuffing out of hope.

Occasionally, he could be folksy, a man of the living room, hot chocolate in hand. More than one judge had heard Lawyer Peterbuoy dispatch eloquence and rest a case with a simple "He was cranky. She was cranky. What are you going to do?"

Turns out, a lot. First, he would tell the accused man that the deal was five years in the pokey or a quick exit from the town. Lawyer Peterbuoy would offer the man a room at his place in the country for a few days. "You can think there. I offer respite."

Few of his clients had ever stretched a neuron thinking and most didn't know what a respite was, but they could sense the terms of the deal and it always sounded okay.

Second, Lawyer Peterbuoy would tell family or friends, if there were any left who cared, that the accused had been offered work and rehab far away.

It was like the setting of a scene in a good movie, although there was more to it than that. Much more.

Lawyer Peterbuoy was a serial killer.

THE RULES OF THIS justice system were odd, and not all of his clients were offered the deal. Some of them disgusted Lawyer Peterbuoy as much as they disgusted everyone else.

If a man, though, beat his mate with fists, caused contusions, bruises, and broken parts, if, that is, he seemed to embrace cruelty as though it were a good-luck charm or a winning lottery ticket, Lawyer Peterbuoy would negotiate him up to his place "like a branch," he wrote in his diary, "into a leaf chopper." He truly meant the expression figuratively.

Were weapons involved, Judge Fieflieber and Lawyer Peterbuoy would flip a coin.

Were weapons involved and actually used, it was all Judge Fieflieber. Lawyer Peterbuoy, apart from being the defense attorney of record, wanted no part of a man who'd punctured his wife with a knife or a bullet or who'd hit her over the head with a baseball bat or a five iron. Those types deserved the long contemplation of adulthood behind hard bars. Word was, they were labeled "brides" in the clink and, following such ceremony as prisoners have time for, learned about the receiving end of spousal abuse. They also tended to do a lot of laundry.

LAWYER PETERBUOY LIVED OUT in the woods on seven hundred acres not far from the Pappadapsikeag River. It was beautiful country, a part of northern Maine that was a scrapbook of verdant excess. Tribes, until a few hundred years previous, had roamed there for a thousand years, eating and living and burying bones.

Upon arrival at Lawyer Peterbuoy's the abuser was hit over the head enough times to render him unconscious, often dead. Following that, he was disposed of, not a hard thing to do within the confines of seven hundred acres. Most of the stories had it that those fellows were just eaten by things.

THERE WERE INTIMATIONS. WOMEN in tough situations would sometimes tell their mates they'd turn them in, thus guaranteeing some kind of oblivion. Everyone knew that. It was an enlightened time and the law viewed a pop to the choppers as a threat to the social order.

The men would laugh, though—a hard thing for an oppressed woman to take—and just say, "Big deal. I'll get Lawyer Peterbuoy. He ain't lost yet."

They were saddened by that, but those who

knew a few things, including Lawyer Peterbuoy with his slight disdain for wisdom, simply said it has never been the purpose of justice to make anyone happy.

Learning

MADNESS

The fourth grade teacher in Quilli, Mrs. Johnson, went to her principal one day and said: "Dornan pulled on me."

Her principle, Mr. Factsampler, a youngish man of thirty-five, said, "He what?"

"He reached up under my dress and grabbed my intimates."

"He did?"

"Yes, sir."

"He'll deny it."

"I know."

"Has he set anyone's hair on fire lately?"

"Not that I'm aware."

"Then live with it."

"Mr. Factsampler?"

"I know."

"Just a note on his sheet."

"Fantasia—we change his sheet, a copy goes to the lawyer. You know that."

"But he did it!"

"Did you encourage him?"

"What?"

"You know how it goes, Fantasia."

WHEN DORNAN CZYCZK STAPLED Honey Tupper-cup's eyelid to the high cheekbone under her eye, the first thing Mr. Factsampler said to Fantasia Johnson was: "Honey's new in school, isn't she?"

"She's new," Fantasia said.

"Talk to her."

ON ANOTHER DAY, MR. Factsampler asked Fantasia Johnson if she wanted him to get her an aide for Dornan Czyczk.

"The last thing he needs is help," she said.

"You know what I mean," he said. "What happened to your finger?"

"Dornan bit it. He bit my fingernail off."

"Is it okay?"

"It is now."

. . .

FANTASIA JOHNSON WAS WELL liked at Quilli Elementary. The first, second, and third grade teachers all knew what she was going through. The third grade teacher, her hair, after the fire, having grown back over the summer break, counseled her, off the record, to keep a record.

"A separate record?" Fantasia asked. "Isn't that against federal law?"

"Do it, honey," she said. Fantasia was still very young.

The upper grade teachers tended to believe they wouldn't have to face Dornan and his disabilities, that something would happen. Fantasia Johnson said she had felt the same way.

AT HER FIRST PARENT-TEACHER conference with Dornan's parents (and their lawyer), Dornan's father was blunt, reciting a speech he'd made before: "So we screwed up the boy. So what? Unscrew him. That's your job."

Mr. Factsampler, as he always did, tried mediation. "It's not a singular thing, Mr. Czyczk. We're all in this and we need your help. We need the family. We need the community."

"He needs a good school," Mr. Czyczk replied.

"I think he has that," Mr. Factsampler said.

"He needs good teachers."

"He has those, too."

"Then do your damn job."

Fantasia Johnson wanted to tell them—off the record—how Dornan had put a pencil all the way through her foot, pinning it to her sandal. (She'd healed.) She'd been going to tell them she felt like Christ without the perks. Ogden Factsampler complimented her on her reticence.

"I just didn't get the chance, Mr. F," she said.

DORNAN WAS AT HIS most unrestrained after the conferences. The next day, during reading, he walked up and down the rows in Mrs. Johnson's classroom squirting Super Glue on the other students. As hands and fingers shot up to cheek or ear or hair to feel out what was happening, they stuck in all those places.

"Dornan," Fantasia Johnson said when she noticed him and saw what was going on, "come up here."

Like some small gunslinger from another time, Dornan approached her, a tube of glue in each hand. Dornan, however, had thought of everything.

Beyond protocol, Fantasia Johnson slapped the young child. Her hand stuck immediately to his cheek—a fact that would later become part of the record: *her* record.

FANTASIA JOHNSON, NO DUMMY either (and still in her late twenties), was offered therapy and accepted the offer. She became nervous and had a note on that put in her file. There were absences, too, sick days, all supported by medical documentation.

The Czycks, who loved their boy, expressed a certain smugness over that. He'd had to leave the hospital with a red cheek from the glue remover. They thought it fine that his teacher was now on notice. Parents had to protect their young.

PROTECTION, HOWEVER, CAN BE a salty spray. Upon her return to the classroom, Fantasia Johnson had an incident with Dornan. Her medication kept her smooth, however, smooth enough that when Dornan thought she was going to send him to the office she took him aside and said, "No. I'm not sending you to the office."

"But you said—"

"I'm sending you to the cafeteria."

"Huh?"

"So they can cut you up and serve you as hamburger."

FACTSAMPLER WAS APOLOGETIC TO the Czyczks, but when Mr. Czyczk said, "Fire her," Mr. Factsampler said, "I can't."

"You can't?"

"She's been under stress, under medical treatment. It's the same law protecting Dornan. She'll be all right, though."

"Protecting Dornan?" Mr. Czyczk said.

DORNAN, AS EVEN THE students noticed, seemed to be losing weight. He talked less and the nasty sparkle in his eye of impending horror was less frequent. Not gone, however. When he ripped the earrings from Honey Tuppercup's ears she turned on him and shoved a calculator in his mouth that knocked out two teeth.

Honey Tuppercup was expelled for that and had to go to the Christian school in Quilli for the rest of the year. On another day, though, when Dornan had spent a good ten minutes during science standing at the blackboard and scraping his nails across it, Fantasia Johnson turned on him and bit every one of his nails down to the quick.

"WE'RE WORKING WITH HER," Mr. Factsampler told the Czyczks. The Czyczks were worried. Dornan no longer seemed himself. Factsampler didn't feel comfortable enough with the Czyczks to tell them how refreshing that was for all concerned.

COMFORT WAS LESS AVAILABLE to the Czyczks, who entered divorce proceedings in the middle of all of this. They filed several formal complaints against Fantasia Johnson but Ogden Factsampler (and eventually the school attorney) said these were health matters and there was nothing they could do. Fantasia Johnson was a nervous woman, but she was young and they were confident she would move out of it.

"Properly speaking," he told them, "I'm not even supposed to talk about her health problems. I just wanted you to know she's not a mean person."

• • •

IN THE FOURTH GRADE, however, the gossip was that Dornan had moved.

"He's living with his mom," someone said, a fact hotly denied by a child who said Mrs. Czyck lived next door to her and she lived alone. Another said he was with his dad, but that was countered by another child who'd had the tip of her tongue pinched off by Dornan. She said his dad was driving a truck now and was gone for weeks at a time.

SMALL TOWNS BREED MORE hope than truth. The truth was that Dornan Czyczk never was seen again and Fantasia Johnson got her nerves back before the school year ended. Ogden Factsampler was happy about that. Good teachers are hard to find in cold northern places.

MURDER

Squis had the food and had been waiting for over an hour, she said, in Hunellia Faulk Ponus Park on the north edge of Quilli, not all that far, Squis had told someone once, from Labrador. She thought that was true.

She was waiting for Dené and Li-Lee who were always late because one or the other of them had to go to the ATM or had to buy cigarettes, which wasn't all that hard, you just had to say "They're for my mother." Dené said her father said that was what they'd always had to say as kids, but he thought they'd just gotten away from it for a long time, until the new laws had come along. He was fond of saying, "It all just goes around."

SQUIS ENVIED DENÉ, WHO was pregnant, and Li-Lee who had a child, a little girl being kept for her by her aunt in St. A de P. Squis thought everyone was so much like everyone else and she was more like everyone else than anyone else that just being something was necessary. God knew, she thought, how in the world Dené and Li-Lee would be able to handle kids, but all Squis had so far was 1350 on the SAT and no one had come up to her wanting to rub her tummy and say "Cool" just because of that.

Since Hunellia Faulk Ponus Park was rarely inhabited by anything other than grosbeaks and geese flopping around the moldy lake it was a good place to meet to talk about the most extraordinary thing—the murder—without having to worry about anyone butting in to say they knew why about what, when everyone knew nobody knew anything about any of it. Sometimes you just had to roll around in bad things and dream about them and jabber into inanity without someone, say, like Squis's mother, who was a physician, ragging you into an unlibelous boredom strangled by facts.

"You brought?" Dené asked.

"Liverwurst for you," Squis said, while Li-Lee hopped on top of the picnic table and sat cross-legged and said, "Fried egg for me?"

"Naturellement."

"You're a princess."

"I am."

"I hate you."

"No you don't."

Dené had pulled apart the two slices of bread of her sandwich and was licking the sausage off it as she reached into her backpack and removed a pint bottle of whiskey.

"Do you know what I heard?" Squis began, but Dené interrupted her and said she had to get some clothes for school.

"This time around—" she began, jutting her abdomen out in an awkward way and smiling.

"Of course!" Li-Lee said.

"—it's a little different."

She said her nipples were itching all the time, too, and Li-Lee said there was stuff you could get for that.

Li-Lee said, "This is a good sandwich, Squis."

SQUIS WAS IN THE middle of a sixteen-ounce tub of yogurt and just said "Thanks" and took the whiskey bottle from Dené.

"Right here, you know," Squis said.

"Here what and what do I know?" Li-Lee asked, then Dené said, "I think murder's cool."

"Dené!" Squis said.

"A perception, you know," Dené said. "It's an infinite power kind of thing."

Li-Lee put the bottle down and said: "A little ol' life and death thing, honey?"

"Off the record?" Dené said.

"Who's keeping a record?" Li-Lee answered.

"I peed forty-six times yesterday."

"Off the record?" Squis said. "I think that *is* a record."

Dené was holding the whiskey bottle over her head and looking at the sun through the amber glass as she said, "It got to be—a—little—erotic?"

She looked at Squis as she said it and Squis, thinking Dené was trying to shut her out of something, said, "They do it all the time now."

"They?" Dené said. "They who?"

"Who they?" Li-Lee countered.

"Some movies," Squis said. "My dad gets these brochures."

"HERE'S WHAT MY MOTHER said," Squis began.

"The doctor's report?" said Li-Lee.

148

"As much as she told me," Squis said.

Dené stood up then, her face scowling under a belch of liverwurst and whiskey, and said, "I have to pee."

"We've done pee," Li-Lee said. "I don't want to do anymore pee."

"It's not yours to do," said Dené, getting off the table. Squis didn't think she was walking any too steadily toward the woods at the park's edge. She rolled a little, but she guessed it was probably the baby rolling.

"AN EROTIC EXPERIENCE?" LI-LEE said as Dené returned.

"Like reading a mutual fund report," Dené answered.

"He cut her toes off," Squis finally said.

"As in," said Li-Lee, "what's for dinner?"

"Your mother told you this?" asked Dené.

"Think what that would do to your shoe size," said Li-Lee. "Or wearing sandals," Dené said. "How would you do that?"

"They don't bury you wearing sandals," Squis answered. "I'm sure they don't."

"I forgot she was dead," Dené said.

"Without death—no murder," Squis said.

"Now I know why you're so smart. Isn't she smart, Li-Lee?"

Li-Lee, wiping her mouth with a napkin from Squis's bag, said, "The bottle's empty."

"Squis, honey," Dené began, "I want to name my baby after you—"

"Really?"

"—only"

"What?"

"—only: Squis. Squis? What is that from? What kind of name is that?"

"My dad—"

"Your dad's name?"

"No. He just calls me that."

"Why?"

Squis smiled at Dené then and reached over and brushed some crumbs from her sweatshirt. "It's because I'm not a virgin," she said.

"You're not?" said Dené.

"You're not?" echoed Li-Lee.

"It was medical," Squis said.

"Isn't it always?" Dené asked. "But 'Squis'?"

"It's just a sound, my dad says," Squis answered. "'Like water on leaves,' I think he said, or 'like sex in the rain.'"

"Your dad?" Li-Lee asked.

"That's all I must say," Squis said.

"Oh my," said Li-Lee.

"A good baby name, though," Dené said. "A good baby name."

Li-Lee, a puzzled look on her face, finally said, "Really good."

Danielle came up to Quincy Faulk Ponus at the school and told him she had eighty-seven thousand dollars in the bank and that she had dual citizenship, American and Canadian. This was at her high school in Digby, Nova Scotia.

Quincy Ponus was a recruiter for the small state university in Quilli. Children told him things about their money. Sometimes, he knew, they told the truth.

"Where do you live?" he asked her.

"Kejimkujik," she said. "That's about five towns into nowhere from here."

She was in grade twelve, an animal quickness to her, brown hair that had some blond messed into it. Peroxide is and is not popular, Quincy thought, but it never goes away.

She had rough, scratched hands, too, and her knuckles looked bruised.

"My father's seventy-one," Danielle said.

"Oh?"

"My mother worked in a sardine factory."

HIS CONSULTS ARE FREE and then he disappears. While the name and address will be faxed by modem to the machine back in Quilli—"You'll get mail from us," he jokes with the students, "until you're around sixty-five"—he is, he knows, ephemeral, less permanent than last week's spiked hair.

Still, he is one of their first experiences with a broader world. They know they are being coded as they speak so they come on rich and they come on powerful. Quincy's the first test but he's not really there. It's like masturbating and then asking, "How was it?"

"I WORK ALL THE time," she said. "I've worked since I was five."

"What do you do?" Quincy asked.

"I rake blueberries. I pick raspberries. Everyone around here is so old, I go into the woods for them and haul out dead trees. It's wet wood."

"They pay you?"

"A lot," she said. "Especially the men. This one guy? He pays me the most when I'm really dirty. He says it shows industry."

"You work hard, I think."

"I always have," she said, but then, "I jog, too. I'm not an athlete. I don't do any sports. I just run whenever I can."

"What do you do in your spare time?" Quincy asked. He was joking, but the joke was often the joking itself: the kids have been told that this thing with the college people is really, really serious.

"None of us," Danielle replied, "has any spare time."

AT HER AGE, QUINCY thought, he had nothing but spare time. It was all extra, uncommitted. There was a freedom to it and that was good. Then it was gone and that was good, too. Too much being free, someone once said, leads to unreasonableness later in life.

"DO YOU HAVE ANY friends?" Quincy asked. This was not a formal interview. Danielle's school was having a college fair and he was in the gym with about thirty other universities, only two of which were American. His table was next to the Royal Canadian

Mounted Police ("'RCMP' is what you *always* say") and he was impressed.

The talk, though, it's always fun to push the kids, to see how awkward they can be as they try to bargain. Besides, unlike Danielle, I had plenty of time.

"One," Danielle said.

"One?"

"One good one. Her name's Beaches."

"Oh."

"She wants to be a massage therapist. Do you have that at your school?"

"No," he said.

"Why not?"

"You don't exactly need a college degree to be a massage therapist."

"I suppose," she said. He kept moving between Danielle and his display of Quilli and the university campus, replacing booklets as students took them. Now and then he would reach over and just brush her forearm with his fingertips, a way of saying, non-threatening, I'm here. I'm listening.

"But you need to be smart," Danielle continued. "Beaches says you have to know nearly everything to do it. You touch bodies, she says, **and** you get people's feelings on your hands. You have to put them some-where."

"That's oddly put," Quincy said. "A funny way of looking at it."

"Not funny." Danielle's eyes, gray as a fog off the Bay of Fundy, suggested she was moving in for a kill. Quincy wondered if he'd confirmed his motel reserva-tion for that night. He was going to Truro.

"Odd, dear," he said. "Strange."

"You don't want to put your hands to your mouth, she says. You'll catch people's feelings like you'd catch a cold."

"Is Beaches here?" Quincy asked.

Danielle ignored the question. "She says you have to put them into history. The feelings. She studies Latin so she can do it. She thinks every massage ther-apist should study Latin. Do you have that?"

"No," he said. "Not many schools do anymore."

"Hm."

That was a grunt. Clearly, I was under assault.

"I thought colleges did everything. Aren't they supposed to?"

"It's expensive."

"So is a bad day. Beaches says she'd charge fifty dollars for a bad day, a hundred for a really bad day, especially if she has to use Greek. She studies Greek, too. Do you have that?"

Quincy, enjoying all of it, enjoying being nailed by this intrepid inquisitor, had a vision of his struggling president fighting—just then—to keep her physics department. "No, we don't," he said.

"SHE HAS RINGLET CURLS," Danielle continued, "and she is not a gracious person."

"Beaches?"

"Yes."

"But she's still your friend?"

"Friend? She's an excellent friend. I am not sure, though, that in matters of hygiene she knows her toe from a tickle. Do you offer that? Do you teach hygiene?"

"We do not teach hygiene, Danielle." Quincy was beginning to feel like a wallflower at the Uglybug Ball. "Look, let me show you, over here—"

"She's a dirty person. I can smell her sometimes. I think it's in her house. Houses shouldn't smell funny but her place does. She and her mom sometimes pee in the Basin. She told me that. Her mother's old, real old."

Annapolis Basin, Quincy remembered. Canadian geography, for a Quilli native, was such a kick.

"I HAVE ALL THAT money," she said again. Irrelevant, was Quincy's first thought. She didn't yet know she could be bought. There were scholarship forms in his catalog case.

"I will be recommending—" he started to say. Danielle interrupted him. She seemed to do that freely, though she was not an abrasive young woman.

"Maybe I should just live," she said. "Can you do that?"

"Permission granted," Quincy said. "What do you mean?"

"Just live," she said. "Get up in the morning and dress. Go to bed at night and undress. Beaches can give me massages and I can eat candy and read Atwood. Do you teach Atwood at your school?"

"I'm sure we do. A writer?"

"How else would I read her?"

"BEACHES HAS A RING through a tooth."

"Fashion has us do many things, doesn't it?"

"Does it? She drilled the hole herself. She thinks I should do it, too. Do you think I should?"

"Danielle?"

"Yes?"

"Do you want to?"

"She says sometimes things test you and you just work it out, even painful things. I don't think I could, not myself. Maybe if she did it to me."

"What grade are you in, Danielle?"

"Twelve."

"How old are you?"

"Seventeen. I might be older, though. I've been working for a long time and that makes you older."

"MY PERIOD STARTED WHEN I was eight," she said. "I had my first baby when I was eleven."

"How many children do you have?"

"None. He died."

"That's very sad, Danielle."

"Not really," Danielle continued. "He wasn't wanted and I didn't know what to do with him. There was no purpose for him in this world. He would have grown up to be grumpy. Probably all the time."

"Do you want to have more children someday?"

"No. I didn't much care for the conception part of it. Beaches says it's awfully primitive."

Danielle kept brushing one hand across her nose and then down across her breast, a gesture that was keeping her nipples erect. Quincy had two chairs behind his table display and he finally invited her back there to sit down. She didn't hesitate at all.

"IS BEACHES OLDER THAN you?" he asked.

Danielle said, placing both hands flat on her legs near her knees, "I'm very old."

"I know that," he said. "I think you are, too."

"Can you study old people at your school? Really old ones?"

"Older than you, Danielle?"

She smiled, her first smile since they'd begun talking, but then she said: "Don't put me on."

"Put you on?"

"Beaches isn't my boss, you know."

"You mention her a lot."

"She's cool."

"Okay."

"She's a fanatic, too. An excellent fanatic."

"About?"

"What?"

"About something. People are usually fanatic about something."

"No."

"Not Beaches?"

"She's just a fanatic."

THE COLLEGE REPS WERE to be at the school for three hours. At noon they would move on to a school in Annapolis Royal. When the bell rang Danielle said she had to go to class and left. As she walked away Quincy stared after her. She was shapely, he thought, even in a teen's wrap: hips that had never played to a crowd, come-along shoulders that had never gone along (she hadn't liked the conception part, Quincy remembered).

Hormones, however—nature's deodorant—had tried hard to protect against too much and in the end Danielle looked tough, looked in fact like she had been working hard and working long.

Quincy smiled as he remembered that phrase. It

was part of their latest advertising campaign and flashed up at him from all his booklets.

AFTER TWO MORE CLASS periods Danielle returned. She was wearing makeup now, a light pink to her lips, a barely conceptual brown eyeshadow. She also had someone with her, a girl, very young-looking, though few teenagers, Quincy knew, look like what they are. Was this Beaches?

"This is Gabby," Danielle said.

"Gabrielle?" Quincy asked.

"Sometimes," she said.

He couldn't see Gabby as being more than eighty pounds. She wore a skirt and low heels, the usual sweatshirt. Not at all undernourished, she looked healthy—simply small; a doll, he thought. He didn't say it.

"You want to study in the States?" he asked.

"No," Gabby said. "Beaches says it's all crime over there."

He laughed then, politely adult. "You're not reading your own newspapers?"

They knew what he was referring to. Just recently a man and his wife had been convicted of murdering young girls. The torture was not new, but videotaping all the excesses had been. They'd been caught when they'd forgotten a tape in a motel VCR somewhere.

"Cheap people," Gabrielle said. "Oil up the gallows."

"You don't have that," Quincy said. "Capital punishment."

"Not now," she answered.

"Do you do that?" Danielle asked.

"Do what?"

"Study that. Hanging bad people."

"No. Not as a whole course of study."

"Too bad."

"Is it?"

"Aberrance," she said. "I could study that. A whole lifetime of people on the freaky side of decency."

"Danielle?" Gabrielle's eyes were wide, teary.

"Beaches told me she killed a cat—with an iron," Danielle said.

"An iron what?" Gabrielle asked.

"Not 'an iron what,'" Danielle answered. "A clothes iron. She ironed it. Scratched her bloody, she said."

"Do you believe her?" Quincy asked.

They both looked at him as though he were too stupid to realize that some things were beyond question.

"It was before I got pregnant," Danielle said. "She was just a child."

"The cat wouldn't have appreciated that," Quincy said. She was telling stories, he was sure of that. But it was all right.

"When you're a child, you're a child," Gabrielle said.

Danielle added, "Maybe those people—was it Ontario?—maybe they were just kids."

"Could have been," Gabrielle said.

"Could have been," Danielle replied. "Kids know a lot about taping, about technology."

"Amazing," Quincy said.

"ARE YOU IN LOVE with Beaches?" Quincy asked. The customer is always right, he thought. Her needs can be filled anywhere so the astute seller is always a sponge until the sale is either completed or it is clear—vivid—that things are going nowhere. *I take from children in my work, my living, so it is no matter if they amuse themselves with me.*

He needed to push things along, he knew—this sale. The morning was almost over.

"Beaches?" Danielle said.

"Beaches?" Gabrielle said.

"This wise person," Quincy said. "Not only do you listen when she speaks, you remember."

"We forget, too," said Danielle.

"You do?"

"A lot," Gabrielle said.

"Beaches says memory is cheap avoidance," Danielle went on. "She says it's like history without all the statues or places we can't go to because we won't let go of where we've been. Beaches has been everywhere."

Quincy thought: This child, Danielle, is a whip and a wit.

"Is there history at your school?" Danielle asked. "You know, like they teach it?"

"Yes," Quincy said. He nearly leaped into the air as he thought of the four hungry professors back home in Quilli who were ready to jump into *this* conversation.

"God, I hate history," Gabrielle said.

"Why?"

"I forget," she said, which seemed to her a quite satisfactory answer.

• • •

GABRIELLE WANDERED OFF TO look at other schools and Danielle stepped close to Quincy. Her breath smelled of tobacco, her skin of sweat. He noticed a line of pale dirt that ran from her neck down into her shirt.

"Beaches had surgery last night," she said.

"Serious surgery?"

"They wanted to put new tubes in her heart," she said. "Veins—something like that."

"It's not uncommon," Quincy said. "Although if you're pretty young—"

"She's been waiting a long time."

"IS SHE ALL RIGHT?" Quincy asked.

"They found pustules," she said.

Quincy smiled: a word right out of history, though he was kind enough not to say anything.

"What does that mean?"

Danielle licked her lips slowly, an absent gesture, automatic. Her tongue was pink from some kind of candy she'd been eating. Quincy thought: breath mint?

"Things growing that don't ever die," she said. "She has cancer of the heart."

"Where is she?"

"She's in Yarmouth. They're going to take her on a ferry to Maine."

THINGS HAD SLOWED, HAD nearly ended. Most of the kids had already drifted off to the cafeteria. Quincy was nearly breathless from Danielle's performance, though he wondered how much was truly her and how much had been prompted, his own words sometimes much too slick.

We do it, we have banners and brash booklets, displays of pictures that convey as much about our own hopes for our campuses as they do any realities. We are, for many kids, a first indication that a world beyond home and school—a world so many of them feel obligated to hate (Is it genetic? I've often wondered)—might actually want them. We pander and joke and cajole, sometimes beg.

In the background always, like an old drunk uncle, is the passionate notion of price.

What do you want from us? they seem to ask, annoyed by that most dangerous combination of emotions: flattery and suspicion.

We don't exactly tell them.

It's not time to grow up, we might say.

Oh?

We can hide you.

No.

Go out there and work right now, make money, marry, buy things—it'll change you. You don't want that.

Yes!

It'll make you mean when you should be clever.

Being mean's all right.

You'll get early wrinkles and drink too much coffee before you're twenty-five.

Oh, yeah?

Women on the bottom, guys on top—that sort of thing.

Way it is now.

It doesn't have to be.

DANIELLE HELPED QUINCY TAKE down his display. She stacked his brochures and slipped his pictures into their big leather envelope. A single, simple gesture, he thought, but it revealed a lot. Danielle knew work and knew when things needed to be done. A little cruelly, he still wondered about the money, the eighty-seven thousand dollars. Tough kids don't give dreams up easily.

"Keep us in mind, Danielle," he said. "It might be time for you to get away."

"Beaches says she might need the money, might need all of it."

"You'd give it to her?"

"She said those tubes drain everything—money, hope, all the lives you've grown to love."

"A lot of things do that. You'd give it all up?"

"For Beaches?"

"For her."

"I'd die right now, this minute."

"She'd want you to do that?"

"That doesn't matter."

"It usually does."

"Not here."

"No?"

"Beaches is my mother. Didn't I say that? I'm sure I did."

"Maybe so."

"That's why I work so hard. It's what you do. I'd be lazy if it weren't for Beaches. I'd be very lazy."

Finally, Quincy thought, identifiable fiction. He didn't believe *that* in her for a minute.

Loss

ANGLES

One night after church Sylvia Rub'ber took himself into the woods and was never seen again in a recognizable state.

There had been no warning. In fact, Sylvia had told several people his life was good. He had sold his farm to a computer expert from Waltham, Massachusetts, for exactly twice what he had hoped he would get. His cirrhosis had cleared up and he was pink again, pink being always the color of choice in northern climes. He had found, too, a room in Quillifarkeag, a small upstairs suite the owner referred to as a "suit," in a house near Hunellia Faulk Ponus Park with heat coming out of the walls and no electric bill that he had to pay.

The house was owned by a woman forty years old, a buxom lady with hair the color of dead tomato vines as Sylvia saw it. She told him the first week that he could sleep with her on Sunday nights because neither of them worked and everyone needed a way to make a new week special.

Sylvia hadn't had sex in ten years and he thought that was an extraordinary way to start a new week, especially since the woman, whose name was Fell, was an active sort who found as much pleasure in him as he did in her. What he liked most about her was her smell—an odd reminder of olives and roses—which he compared with good cooking that didn't have to be paid for.

He was happy, he told people. This caused a certain amount of worry since northern people distrust happiness. Its curse is that of a fine possession that can only be lost, whereas misery presents nothing but endless opportunity.

Sylvia was discrete about Fell, but a single man at sexual ease is an obvious target. He knew this, but he also told people he was happy waiting for something bad to happen. He didn't think it would take very long. It never did.

THAT SUNDAY NIGHT, AFTER church, Sylvia went home and found Fell with her old husband. They were in the kitchen and the man had a smile like an airport beacon. It seemed to flash on and off whenever he opened his mouth. To Sylvia, it looked like something you'd want to control with tape or rope.

"We are going to have a late baby," the man told Sylvia. The man smiled. Sylvia, like so many farmers, was quick with math and knew you couldn't have two fathers of the same child in one room. Two mothers, what with science and all—Sylvia read a great deal— but not two fathers. The real father wasn't smiling at all.

Sylvia was religious enough, and still flush with the evening's service, to know that a child should have no false fathers before it. That was, almost completely, what was wrong with the country.

Sylvia couldn't handle being anyone's problem, especially not the problem of a child who hadn't even been born yet. That's what was later said, that he knew this.

HE WENT BACK TO his farm that night, to a tree that was wonderful. It was on a part of the farm that the computer expert didn't go to because he only wanted the farm to have it. Very new money always buys very old land, someone said. The farm was pretty and you could see Canada. Sylvia once said you could see Labrador from his farm, though you could not.

The tree was an oak and it had a long root sticking half in the ground and half out and about the width of a telephone pole. The root ran out from the bottom of the tree for thirty or forty feet and a big hole had been gouged out beneath that root, a hole big enough to hold a man. Sylvia sharpened the end of a big stick and jammed it into that hole, just beneath a big branch overhead. The stick stuck out at a forty-five degree angle. Sylvia knew angles, too, because he was a farmer. Forty-five degrees is the angle at which things, living things, die. Everyone knew this. Precision is important in places where it is cold.

SYLVIA CLIMBED THE BIG branch over the hole and squatted, as farmers often do. He looked like he was ready to carry on a conversation with friends, maybe, a Diet Coke (his favorite) in one hand while the other hand was left free for gesturing, for making points. You make points, he knew, and people thought better of you. What people thought had always been important to Sylvia.

He carefully tied his bare ankles to the branch with stout rope. Then he stood and swung backward and downward. He traveled in nearly half of a perfect circle. He could hear his ankle bones snap even as the stake crashed through his spine and poked his heart out through his sternum. Sylvia had known exactly how it all would happen and that there would be no pain.

No one went looking for him. They cared, but they knew things had been going too well for Sylvia and you just didn't want that to happen, not in a northern clime. Precision can have too much said for it, but Sylvia had seen that some angles needed to be changed to circles and he had done that just fine.

Eventually, as his meat and his clothes went away into the air and his foot bones slipped their loose nooses, he relaxed into a dignified cuddle around the stake and in the hole. He had planted himself and it was a nice job.

PARENTS

Standing near the old linen factory, its four stories of windows overlooking the St. John, Claire waited for Stephen King.

The river had frozen weeks before, then thawed and froze again—and again and again—until it looked like the boulder wash at the foot of a glacier, great ice rocks that would crack and scream like hurt animals in the spring, huge gashes that had refrozen so many times the surface looked the work of a surgeon gone mad or stupid. Later in the season, with the frozen and melting debris fighting for position in the loosening current, the river would begin snapping back, snatching a house here, a car or truck there, a house being the more dramatic instance, yielding slowly to its own abduction, the roof bouncing, walls sagging, the cellar filling with water—later to freeze and crack the foundation walls.

Claire was standing near the old sign with its odd

promise—WELCOME OR NOT, IT'S UP TO YOU—wearing her cherry slicker over her down coat and stamping her feet in the gravel and frozen mud. Mostly, she remembered, the river ripped at the widows.

On those sunny days after the river had receded, where even the destruction looked normal and cheery, another two or three of the older women would be taken to Thibodeau's and the bus and the drive down to Quilli and the airport. Claire had heard the conversations too many times.

Where are you going, Evelyn?
I'm all right.
Where are you going?
I'm fine once more again.
To your daughter? Is that where? To your son?
I'm good, though.
Evelyn? Eugenia? Larisse?

THOSE TIGHT LITANIES WERE always in French, the women with their backs straight, their chins pointed anywhere but down, good women discovering that pride had nothing to do with character and everything to do with how and where you placed your body, right here—now.

Claire turned away from the road and the old sign and walked toward the building, her building now, its ugliness hers along with each and every brick.

There were ways to crack that ugliness, ways to bring the building back to when it hadn't been ugly, when it had been "the women's factory" tucked right here into the side of the hill with a wooden door for the main entrance that was just like the wooden door to the kitchen of any number of houses in town, if not all of them.

So many mornings she'd walked here with her mother, the two of them alone for two streets, then slowly picking up others on the way, her mother tall and slim the way Claire was not, tall enough, in the winters especially, to be doused with the first sun, her brown hair thin as a spider's web and taking fire with that early light. She would hold Claire's hand for most of the way, her hand warm but never still, jerking Claire's arm around as she chatted and gestured, recounting the news from the television the night before, pointing out inconsistencies, framing sadnesses that she, her mother, if not Claire, ought to remember, but she certainly would, giving her precise instructions on what needed to be thrown into the oven at three, telling her to invite Cynthia or Katy over so she wouldn't have to eat alone, eating alone not at all good for a child's digestion.

A chain was suspended from a bracket on the door to an identical bracket on the door frame, its ends joined by a fat padlock. Claire had the key, but with the wooden steps having been stolen years before, she was still, even on her toes, an inch short of being able to reach the lock. Perhaps Mr. King could reach it— she'd heard he was tall—or she could roll her car up close or they could find a log to roll over to the door. There were lots of ways it could be done.

THERE HAD BEEN NO linen made in the linen factory during Claire's lifetime, nor during her mother's lifetime either. That business had blown away at about the same time that the Depression had blown quietly, hardly noticeably, through the town. The near-war years had brought a certain happiness when a condom company bought the factory and began production. When the war itself started, the women were already in place, working twenty-four hours a day, the women's factory a glowing outpost against disease up there on the St. John. Later, when Vietnam was an issue and condoms were not, Claire's mother worked there as the janitor. More than anything, though, it seemed like those decades came and went like great chunks of ice, falling all over everything, spectacular in significance, and disappearing in a slow thaw.

CLAIRE THOUGHT ABOUT THE business at hand, this transaction with Stephen King. She smiled when she thought of that and tried to remember who had described him to her, the realtor perhaps, who didn't know him and probably heard about him from a friend down in Bangor who'd gotten whatever *she* knew from the tabloids.

What might she say to such a man?

"Good morning. I'm Claire Prêtmaison and I'm incredibly ruthless."

Very well, she thought. I might be "cute," too, or even "adorable," most of that having come from my father, a short man, bearded (some resemblances end) or not, depending on where he stood with respect to the border at a given time, a short and altogether bouncy man, dynamic, a lover of food and the owner of an old Corvette, a peacemaker, or so he had hoped. Like all the hired guns back then, though, the cow-boys, the chaps in chaps, not the hippies chanting their way to sobriety, but the tough ones like, she thought, daddy, they'd met ends and the acquaintance had been short and rich.

A CAR WAS COMING down the highway and Claire thought it must be him. Certainly, only a man like Stephen King would do business on a Sunday morning. Claire wondered if he would bring his wife. She had heard they were close.

QUIKTUPAC, NORTH OF QUILLI, had never been anything more than what it was then, a place where the highway had either to end at the river or begin curving southward, the thinnest of strings holding northern Maine onto the rest of the state, or so it looked on a map. Quiktupac had always existed without portfolio or prestige—an Indian town "after all," the Maliseet living more bad history than most people ever learned in school—some money being made from logging or the various owners and products of the women's factory, or trickling down like an icy rain from Washington, D.C.

But most of its livelihood had come in a more transient fashion, as a haven for political tourists and, on occasion, outright lawbreakers, anyone with a need to stand in one spot and, breathing deeply—sighing sometimes, relaxing, blowing it away—maybe juggling some coins in the pocket or leaning restfully against a spouse, stare off into the nearby nothingness of Canada, a nothingness that had the appeal of the back door to a house where a domestic dispute was going on, where there were shouts and tears, perhaps hitting, rage, a back door where a calmer air could almost be seen. It was a fine escape, reassuring to such a degree it had rarely to be used. That was how most people she had known had thought of Canada. It was not a complimentary view, but it wasn't bad either. Quiktupac was quiet, even desolate, but it was no frontier.

There were no criminals in Quiktupac just then, Claire's father being among the most recent and possibly the last, possibly even the first in many decades and he was gone, his crime having to do with rules more than laws, with things not done more than things done capriciously or outrageously. His first crimes anyway, Claire thought, life not having been kind enough to sort out—which was why Mr. King was coming—his latter ones.

Winters were hard in Quiktupac, and times were hard and summers were short, as was money, and the men left. It had, largely, become a women's town and the women were proud of that, although they were always careful to make sure people understood this wasn't some nineteenth-century cow town people were talking about, some bunch of soddy yentas toothless at twenty with fingernail grime going up to the first knuckle.

Claire's parents had discovered Quiktupac in the sixties, Claire's mother driving the small U-Haul while her father followed in the Corvette, her father continuing on even after her mother had stopped, finding, Claire had always supposed, a looser air up there in Canada, a looser life or maybe better food, maybe another woman. Perhaps, she had sometimes thought, there were even some Québecois half sibs running around up there whom she really ought to meet someday—when there was time.

THE CAR WAS BLACK and impressive and Claire expected that. Slowly, it came off the road and onto the gravel, a loud crunch lifting off the road and into the air, the car fitting right in with the silver-gray landscape where everything was clean and trimmed of any excess, harsh and frosty, metallic.

The driver's door opened and the driver got out. The driver dressed in black, very neat and tidy Claire thought: a leather cap, a black wool coat, black trousers, and black shoes with soles that seemed too thick for the patent-leather uppers.

The driver said, "Good morning, ma'am," as she stepped nervously over the crunch ice, and Claire nodded. Stephen King emerged from the car, the brown bombardier jacket, unzipped, seeming casual enough, the khaki slacks, too, and the turtleneck and the Dexter ducks.

He wasn't tall, either, not at all. He was wearing tiny, wire-rim sunglasses, which he took off right away as he said, "Mrs. Prêtmaison?"

"It's 'Miss,' Mr. King. Thank you."

He put the sunglasses back on. "This is the place?"

"Not much to it, is there?" Claire said. "I think I told you that on the phone."

"Yes, you did. Simple places, simple events. You seemed awfully worried about my time. That was nice."

"It has become valuable time."

"I suppose," he said. "Oh"—he turned toward the young woman at the door then, the driver, losing his footing for an instant on the ice, one knee dipping— "this is Belle. She works for me. Very hard, I might add."

Claire let the compliment register, then said, "Let's go inside."

She turned to walk to the door, but King put his hand on her arm and asked: "Has the place been cleaned up?"

"What do you mean?" said Claire.

"I meant after—"

"Oh. Well—there really wasn't anyone to do that. It's a small town, you know, just some people, a few people."

"Yes. I know."

"But it's been over thirty years, Mr. King. Thirty years."

"Of course."

THE THREE OF THEM rolled a small log up to the entryway and Belle, the tallest, took the key from Claire and stood on the log to remove the lock and chain. The door swung open easily then. Claire ex-

pected the squeak of rusted hinges, but the door
opened by itself and tapped gently against the inner
wall.

They were in a short corridor with one room off to
the left lined with boards holding coat hooks—a
good many of them missing—while to the right was
the office, a room ten by fifteen feet containing nothing more than a light cord dangling from the ceiling.
There was no trash, no broken or rotting office furni-
ture strewn about, no old papers, no work orders, in-
voices, ledger sheets, memoranda, or other intimacies
of the work life gathering dust and fading on the floor.
How lifeless such things always seemed in production,
yet how warm they might have seemed now. Not
cleaned, she told him; he hadn't asked if it had been
emptied.

She remembered going through her parent's papers
and feeling pleased at how organized they had been,
especially since their financial condition had always
been so simple. There had been no investments, no
retirement plans, no insurance, just electric bills—
always paid on time—gas or oil bills, phone bills, rent
receipts, checks filed by number and everything else
organized by date and nothing thrown away, parts or

repairs for the Corvette, medical bills including the complete and itemized cost of her mother's hysterectomy. Claire had been shocked when she'd noticed the eighteen dollar charge for circumcision following her own birth, and she'd wondered if her parents had noticed that and contested it the way they'd contested everything else, always, for as long as Claire could remember, contesting the rule of law, the rule of church, the rule of history, and the price of milk in year after year of frenzied discussion in town after town, always talking, her father red-faced in tie-dyed T-shirts, his mustache wet with spit and wine.

Rooms. The next one, on the right, was the bathroom, the door still on it, which she didn't want to open, not yet, not quite this soon, preferring to follow Mr. King and Belle into the main floor main room, which, stripped though it was, was still interesting with odd-looking overhead brackets, identical fixtures forming a pattern in one spot, a different pattern in another, the machines or work stations long since gone, but the leavings looking like some kind of chalk outline of where a certain kind of life had congregated, had made things: linen, rubbers, war gear— what looked like little railroad tracks curling around through most parts of the big room, long strips of the metal rail, though, gone.

Mr. King, she thought, would have to like this, the tall windows especially, the counterpoint to a certain gloom, light entering the sacred and the sweaty, the shadows where good people had winked and whispered and shared endearments and plans and the heady relief of work along with the harsh aches of labor.

Belle, however, seemed more interested, King just standing there taking it in while Belle moved quickly to the center of the room like a dancer in the dust, walking one of the rails for a dozen feet, going quickly over to one of the windows to rub the grime off and see what was out back, which was not much, Claire remembered, although she followed Belle to the window and together they opened it, the window being only heavy and not at all hard to open.

"There's not much to see," Belle said. "It's almost like a wall." The hill rose steeply outside and was thick with brush and trees.

"You can see in, though," Claire said.

"Into what?" asked King.

"I mean from out there. You can see in, even up to the fourth floor. We used to do that, some of us—my friends."

Which had been, for a long time, a forgotten thing, the cool nights of summer when there would be a knock on the door and Cynthia—sometimes Katy, usually Cynthia, not crying exactly, but lonely many times with the women's factory working three shifts and Claire's and Cynthia's parents almost always working the same two shifts, till midnight, maybe Katy or Cynthia had eaten alone and of course the digestion couldn't handle that, the two girls trying to find something to do for an hour until the unspoken imperative intruded and together they would walk to the factory at nine, stopping well before it where the path began its slow, curving rise around the back of the building, the two of them certain each time that this was a daring, even a new, thing, the well-worn nature of the path not suggesting for a moment that maybe others had gone before.

They would sit then, after a time their locations becoming quite precise, Claire, at one spot, where she could see her father working on the first floor, and Cynthia, not that far above her, looking in, given the nature of physics and optics and angles, on her mother on the third floor.

Cynthia could never figure out where her father was, and the clandestine aspect of the adventure wouldn't allow for any close questioning at home about his work area, but Claire's mother, the janitor, seemed to be everywhere, a gadfly, an interruption with rags and juices, in the waves of motion, the cycles of activity, that swept or alternated from one end of a floor to another, people seeming to stand, almost reverently, for a time over here, then to be bending over and feverishly active on something over there, a harmony, a dance, almost a drama beginning on the fourth floor and working its way back and forth until they would lose sight of it in the sharpness of their angle looking down to the first floor, peaceful evidence of their own survival being wrested from the night for an hourly wage—except for Claire's mother, popping into and out of the rituals with dimly seen tools, implements, standing on ladders, tables, bending over, kneeling on the floor.

They had noticed, one time, and had both watched, her kneeling on a table somewhere near their windows on the second floor, scrubbing something, two buckets on the table by her side, rags flying all over, and had seen a big man, a fat, bearded man wearing overalls and a bright headband around his forehead, his long hair looking floppy and stringy, standing near Claire's mother, talking, laughing, one hand moving constantly through his hair until finally he put that hand on her butt, moving it up and down to where the skirt was moving with his hand, pictures of long thigh shooting up to the girls as they watched and looked at each other, a funny, nervous fear not far from being voiced by both of them, a few people inside in the area, too, seeming to notice something, whispering, looking as though they didn't like what they saw, until Claire's mother rose off of her elbows and, kneeling there, head to head with the man—one of the Cyr family, Cynthia had told Claire later—talking and gesturing rapidly, she finally reached over and slowly pulled the headband down over the man's eyes and—Claire's mother was left-handed—popped him hard on his mouth with her fist.

He'd pulled his headband off then and, following an odd bit of gesturing that the girls later decided had been the removal of a tooth from his mouth, hit back, a clean blow that seemed hardly to extend his arm at all, but a response, still, that left Claire's mother flat on her back on the table.

"I SUPPOSE," CLAIRE CONTINUED, "we were resolving some deep need to connect with our parents, but it didn't seem like that at the time. We were just curious about what they did, about the simple doing—this and that and how did it go?"

Claire wondered if she should have told that story to Mr. King, if he would want it for this big project that was his next, this thing about women in removed areas, this big thing since everything Mr. King did was a big thing.

"Of course you were," Belle said, Claire letting that slip of condescension roll away as the two of them pulled the window back down.

"Mr. King," Claire said from across the room, "the other floors are pretty much identical to this one, but you're free to look if you like. The stairs are—" She turned to look then, feeling as though there was something obvious going on that only she was missing, looking off to the four corners, looking up, puzzled.

"Not obvious," King said, Belle walking off to the side to where several smaller workrooms had been partitioned off, looking in each and then nodding over to King a soft "nope."

"It's all right," King said to Claire. "I can't imagine why they would be different. The bathroom, though. Where is that?"

Claire hesitated, wanting to say that you don't want to see that, that the theme of this big story might start to unravel in there—no women allowed: the can, the jake, the crapper, the kybo, the pisser. Mostly, the women on single shift did not go to the bathroom. They just did not do it.

For those on the double, it was different. First came dinner out on the loading dock: half sandwiches, cans of juice, plastic containers of leftovers from meals made, but not eaten, at midnight—chicken, meatloaf, cold chili, cold stew, endless salads. Always, one of the Gagnon boys would be there, overseeing, supervising yet friendly, stiff, awkward, amused, listening to the dirty jokes of tired women, gaining some sort of spiritual jointure from the belches and all the sighs of ache and strain, accepting bites, morsels, tastes, along with the careful insults, slipping out at exactly the same time each night to unlock the bathroom, returning a moment later to announce quietly, "You can pee now."

"It's over there," Claire said. "By the office, the front door."

"And there was only one?" he asked. "Really?"

"That's what my mother always said."

"She would have known?"

"She cleaned them," Claire said. "I mean—it. She cleaned everything since she was the janitor."

"So she would have had a key?"

"Of course. That's how everything, how it got started."

King and Claire had walked slowly back to the hallway by then, Belle staying behind in the big room and still trying to find the way upstairs.

"I don't know," he said.

"Excuse me?"

"You said on the phone that your father worked here, too?"

"Off and on," Claire said. "There were always some heavy things to be done that Criq said only a man could do."

"Criq?"

"Criq Gagnon. The old man, the owner. He's still alive, but he must be ninety now."

As he had been then, Claire remembered, old and

tall and always "Creek" when her mother said things, and she was always saying things, Criq sounding elfin, mischievous, maybe kind, Creek the boss, Monsieur, Sir.

"C'est votr' kid?"

"Oui, bub," her mother had said.

"Je ne comprends this 'bub,'" he'd said.

"Je regrette, sir. Um—shit. Claire, go on home."

"I WAS THERE THAT night," Claire said. King was in the bathroom, his arms stretched out to touch two of the walls, his voice like a drawing in the shadows. She had never told anyone that, and for a moment she was afraid she'd given something away before she'd even set the scene. She thought it incredibly important that this be told to Mr. King just right.

"But wasn't it—?" Belle's voice came at Claire from behind her and she was startled. "I'm sorry," Belle said. "The one man, though, he would have been your father?"

"He was."

"The one who died."

"What?" Claire asked. Belle had leaned her head and shoulders into the doorway looking for Mr. King.

"The man?"

"Seventeen of them died, you know," Claire said. "You did know that, didn't you?"

SHE HAD LEFT WHEN her mother told her to, had walked around the back and up the hill not far at all, enough to be unseen in the brush, high enough to see into this same floor although to see nothing clearly. Her mother had helped Cynthia's mother—who was seven months pregnant—down the stairs and over to the bathroom, and then Claire's mother had opened the door for her. Claire had seen that, and had seen the tall Criq come out of the office and stand there, looking in the door, a long stick in his hand and Claire's mother nearby, all of this seeming a point of some interest while, across the remaining sweep of window, her father, in the middle of the room with a good line of sight to her mother, was walking slowly over to Criq and Cynthia's mother and his wife, not there exactly as Criq hauled Cynthia's mom out of the bathroom by her hair, her dress not quite on and shifting around so that even in the distance Claire could see the bulging whiteness of the pregnancy, all of that fairly humiliating with Criq both pulling and pushing Cynthia's mother toward the front door and hitting her with the stick at the same time, Claire's father finally at a point where he could see what was happening, approaching with his arms stretched out and high in the air, like he was trying to calm everyone down.

Claire assumed her father was talking or shouting but that was like assuming he was breathing. Across that first floor, too, some of the women had stopped working and were walking slowly toward the front area to see what was happening, to see Criq holding Cynthia's mother by the hair, the woman half-dressed and bent over, the stick on hold up in the air for a moment, until her dad seemed to take a blow from the old man right on his face and that stopped him just at the moment when two of Criq's sons emerged from the office—good-looking business-men, probably in their forties, Claire recalled, always well dressed, clean-shaven—one of them carrying a shotgun.

"So how long did this go on?" King asked.

"How long did what go on?" Claire said. "There wasn't any 'this' that just began and ended. My dad grabbing the stick was one 'this,' but then the Gagnon son fired the shotgun."

"He shot? Why?" Belle asked.

"They said it was a warning, to prevent things from getting out of hand, and I suppose that was another 'this.' They said he fired straight into the floor. It wasn't quite straight, though, because it took Cynthia's mother's foot off, disintegrated it, according to the coroner."

"Oh, Lord," King said.

"Large craziness," said Belle. "She died then?"

"No. It looked so strange, though, to a child, I mean I am trying to give you a child's history, you know—what a child saw, like paper people or caricatures. From where I was it was this group of people apparently just talking, gestures, smiles, the usual trash of talk. Suddenly one of them falls against my father and then he and my mother are all bent over and backing into the bathroom, dragging Cynthia's mother, several of the women following them inside.

"I didn't actually see Criq leave the scene, but a few minutes later he appeared only feet from where I was out back, Cynthia and I on the hill. He was a shaky old man, that's for sure, having a hard time getting his fly open as he walked up to the brush line and urinated. He was talking to himself, in French naturally, and crying, just a big old man crying and I remember that, then talking to me—he must have been, must have been looking right at me when he said, "Is you, bub?"—and finally turning away and walking over to his Buick in back there and leaving, probably passing the sheriff's car as it drove up since the two deputies were entering the building as I walked around to the front.

"I was worried, I suppose, scared, very unsure about what I had seen, wanting to walk into the bathroom because I was certain my parents were in there along with Cynthia's mom, but the Gagnon boys were there talking with the deputies, talking really loud, one of the deputies going over to the bathroom door several times and pressing his ear against it, then stepping back, loosening his tie, rubbing his palms against his pants, the boys and the deputies then gathering in this circle around the bloody patch on the floor. This was just as I ducked inside the coatroom right there. There was a hole in the floor and bits of foot around it, a Gagnon boy and a deputy kneeling, all of them talking, talking fast, I guess trying to talk the whole thing through or away. Maybe they didn't talk long enough, or maybe they didn't know what to say."

"WHAT YOU NEED TO see in this, Mr. King," Claire continued, "is the ordinariness of it. There was no adventure, no drama, no pleadings for life or rescue attempts or bargains being made. That's why I'm asking you to find something to understand in this since to me it's like talking about lunch or sweeping the front porch or here are three interesting things I found in my pockets."

One of the deputies, she said, walked over to the door and fired through it once, moving back the few feet to the others to talk some more. The other one then did the same, except that just as he did so two of the women from the floor walked up—remember, work was still going on and with the noise and all nobody could have known what was happening—their arms loaded with the floppy, dangling parts of something, and the deputy and one of the Gagnon's shot them both.

"You've lost me," Belle said, moistening her finger and rubbing it over a scuff mark on her shoe. "Why would they have done that?"

"That's easy," said Claire, "although, remember, I was ducked inside the coatroom and mostly afraid, at least before the shots, that someone would find me in a place where I didn't belong. But I stuck my head out a few times—only once after the first shots were fired—and saw it."

"Saw what?"

Claire stopped then and smiled at the two of them, a sad smile of remembrance and confusion. She glanced around the room and pulled the cherry slicker tighter around herself, trying not so much to stay warm as to hold things, something, closer, saying finally, "Your reason for being here."

Belle said, "Mr. King?"

"I know," King said.

Claire thought: This is where we all part company with me, where the Republicans and the empiricists scoff, where the damaged child is seen to be still lurking within, its face twisted now and old, leveraged against the world too often for moods gone sour.

"Go on Ms. Prêtmaison," King said. "I'm listening." He was beginning to sound impatient. Claire wondered how you could sleep when your every waking moment was worth thousands of dollars.

"Excuse me," Claire said. "I've never told this to anyone before."

"I understand," he said.

"I mean," Claire continued, "it's like you're the witness though you were never there. But if it all suits you, you'll have it, of course you will, and do whatever it is you do with such things."

"Please," King said. "You were there and you saw things. Something—what?"

"It's why I called you," she said. "You know, let's get this thing out and told once and for all. It's something people's kids do and I own the building now, and the land. There is quite a large piece of land here in spite of the building's being jammed onto the road.

"There's a woman's group, a small foundation I think, that wants to buy it. They like its remoteness, its removal from common paths. They say they'd make it a living place, a place to which certain people could come, a home, in a sense, but a spiritual thing, too— a collection like a museum, yet living and constantly changing."

"That sounds like a wonderful idea," Belle said.

"Does it?" Claire replied. "For decades women labored here without thinking they were part of anything more than a short life lived sadly in a place where dreams never come true. Welcome to anywhere, huh? It just was that way, and for all of it, in the end, all you get is—the devil. Why would anyone celebrate that?"

"You told them this?"

"I'm telling you this." Claire continued, "I wouldn't want it told as truth anyway since she moved so slowly and you'll need to speed her up, Mr. King. Quite slowly, quite unexcitably—something of a craftswoman, really. Or maybe she sensed the unbelief, the work that needed to be done in a factual time. Or maybe I'm as crazy as a peach in strawberry jam. You'll have to work that out even though I believe in craziness for all the thousand names we call it anymore. Yet it was craft, fine and highly detailed, going on there. Craft and command—she directed things and did a good job, efficiently and smoothly. So much of what I saw that day made sense only as I got older, how one by one so many were called and then cut down, the women naively walking up to see what was going on because even the gunshots didn't sound like what they might have expected and the increasing numbers of them lying all about looked like some curious drill, an exercise, something not to be feared but of which to be cooperatively a part. Now and then she looked in on me, Mr. King, bending in around the door and practically getting nose to nose with me, smiling, nodding her head like she was asking for approval, then stepping quietly back into the hall to continue the work, slowly, methodically, with care and terrific attention to detail. Cynthia's mother, for example, gave birth in the bathroom and she, not Cynthia's mother, eliminated that birth, then gave a gun to my father—the peacemaker, the draft dodger with the Corvette—don't forget that, Mr. King—and said, 'Go slowly until you get the hang of it. Then go slower.'"

"Curious," King said, sitting sideways on the toilet and leaning back against the wall. "You're talking about your mother?"

"That's not clear," Claire said. "Now, my dad—that is, he enters, like somebody had just given him a new golf club or baseball bat, a few hefts, a sighting down for trueness, a brush, a touch, a feel. This was a man who used to read *Winnie the Pooh* to me in Latin, by the way. What is the old saying? 'Some men are born to greatness, with others the devil simply says "You'll do.'" She was diligence, you know, and method and persistence and the women fell so hard and fast I think this place was meant to be a release of sorts for things that had nowhere else to go. That's why you can go back thirty years to the newspapers—that's what Belle does for you, doesn't she? The research?—and find hardly a mention of this, nor will you find any of it in recent labor histories because this had nothing to do with that, with working conditions or who can go to the bathroom or when and where. Maybe an old man's vision of things was tied up in it but who'd ever think of that as being new? I think sometimes killing just has to happen, that there's a sloughing off of something and a molting into something else. I saw it in my mother's eyes when she looked in on me and when it was over I saw it in the coverup, in the silence, like nothing had happened that wasn't supposed to have happened except that now a lot of people, mostly kids, had to be cared for and we were—with Criq's money—cared for and educated."

Claire finally said, "There's something a man of your reputation, your connections, can do here, Mr. King. And then I must bring this place down. I would think you'd have to start with the women—

probably end with them, too, certainly with my mother, since this was her performance, her *time* as it used to be put, although somewhere in the middle should be this man with the red Corvette. Him you'd want to make dubious and a shirker, a man with a loud voice and a short attention span. I shouldn't, however, be telling you your business."

THAT'S ALL THERE IS to it, Claire thought, as she stood outside and watched Belle and King drive away. It had been a good morning's work a long time in coming, a work, if you wanted to look at it that way, of plodding thoroughness and careful culturing. The rest, now, belonged to time and thought, to whatever amalgam of circumstance and inspiration might move that famous brain. She—had she really used the word "devil" in referring to her mother?—would be pleased, since Stephen King was the master of, well—call it: the last thing found in everything that people do, the desperation, perhaps, the clear hope.

Claire got into the old Corvette then and started the engine, thinking that somehow the purple cloud rising out of the old motor was appropriate indeed.

FIRE

Ordway Fallgren, like most people, had a secret life. That much was known, although it was known in the way that most indifferent gossip is known: the raised eyebrow, the sly smile of a stranger. A skinny man, roughly shaven, said to be anywhere from nineteen to thirty-five—no one ever remembered him as a boy in Quilli—he was always recognizable in his trench coat and his knee-length rubber boots. He was said to be employed near the river in old town but no one was ever sure what he did.

But he had a way with a joke for a Methodist man. He knew good music and could help people understand what was happening in the cities. One time—this was not his secret—he told Poison Gorelick down in Bud's Bar that he'd like to fall in love with a good man but he couldn't find any.

Poison had told him: "My sister's been dressing in men's clothes for a long time now. Could that be close?"

Ordway joined a long line of people who at one time or another had told Poison Gorelick he didn't quite understand something.

THAT HE HAD LOVED in unusual ways was not his secret either. There had been good women—at least three—in the sixties age group, who had given him home and bed (usually their own) during times when he seemed to need it. Rent was never mentioned, but Ordway would keep pantry and refrigerator well stocked during his stays.

Ordway was courteous to the women and a considerate lover. He knew about the options in life, knew how they could split and diversify like a good stock fund and how the end result was always the same: success or failure. Either result, he knew, was highly addictive.

ORDWAY FALLGREN WAS A poet. That was the secret, the thing no one knew about him until the Methodist Church burned down. His poetry—of a narrative sort—was of generous quality. A lot of it had been published in the places where poets go to publish their work. Those were not places where a Quilli would ever go to read anything, but Ordway Fallgren, like most poets, knew that.

He had never told anyone about his poetry because it had never come up. He was glad of that, too, since Quilli was something like a goose with loose feathers: he plucked liberally from the charm and the meanness and the good bodies of older women, plucked from the histories, too, all the nutty French and the nutty Indians and the nutty Brits, plucked with his mind in a free fall so that things landed where they had to land—the truth in his work not necessarily related to the truth of what had been plucked. In a practical sense, he also decided that if the goose ever discovered that its backside was out there naked and pale to the world, he didn't want to be known as the "plucker who run us all down."

People who do needlepoint, Ordway knew, often felt the same way.

UNTIL, THAT IS, THE fire in his own Methodist Church that sent Fantasia Johnson way up to the top of the steeple trying not to die: until that night he'd been content to let his work be just what it was wherever it was.

The fire had been started by two drunken men who'd gotten to that point in a boozeout where only sex or fire remained as things to do. Had they known Fantasia Johnson, a teacher once, until she'd run afoul of certain rules, a friend of Ordway's who sometimes helped him down by the river—had they known Fantasia was sleeping in the church that night because she'd run out of medication they might have tried to pick her up. They were not evil men, not men who could rape a young woman of tenuous nerves. They would have just thought her an adventure less smelly than fuel oil.

THEY WERE NOT, HOWEVER, thinking men and they set fire to the church with Fantasia in it.

Ordway did not rescue Fantasia (directly, though a publisher would later push him in that direction)— nothing like that got him nailed in for good to the Quilli book of "songs, memories, and old contracts" (a newspaper account).

He was, however, mistaken for one of the volunteer firemen on several occasions, his trench coat, rubber boots, and the general smoky night leading to that assumption.

Plus, it was said, he was everywhere—not in the way, but just all over the place, his coattails flying around, his hair disheveled, a man, they said, taking a constant measure of the inferno and talking, talking it up, talking it around, saying that he understood this fire and that he had a "handle" on it and that he was better than it.

It was an odd way of talking, but then other people were talking, too, and some of that talk was odd, fire directions and people all over the place, lots of small heroisms like the saving of some old stained-glass windows, and a lot of people working very hard, six fire departments, the two Quilli day-shift cops and the one night-shift cop, Trooper Val Dooble from the state troopers, everyone dramatically trying to pull ordinary business out of the high drama of frenzied heat and the ruinous ripping, snapping, bouncing destruction.

WHICH IS WHERE ORDWAY Fallgren came into the one simple story that was ultimately the real fire story—Ordway like some nasty bird trying to feed off grand food sitting on a hot stove, doubts crowding out the sheer iambic joy of conflagration as he remembered talking to Fantasia Johnson and tried to recall what she'd said, talking, he knew, about children all the time, the whole story of her disastrous teaching career known to him, talking about being a child of God and having nowhere to sleep, although Ordway, with something of a Hegelian mood dropping down on him like a German chocolate cake, thought she might have said she was just a child of her time, the two of them having gone together to that very burning church on a number of occasions, just trying to feel as best they could what it was like in the center of things and not always on the edge of things, the cold edge of endless opportunity where a wrong step could turn you into bone dust on the rocks below.

Besides, Ordway was in love with Fantasia. As he told her once, "I'm a poet. How could I *not* fall in love with a woman named Fantasia?"

ALL OF THESE THINGS were streaking around in Ordway's head as someone finally came up to him in the street and said, "Hey. Be careful. What are you doing here?"

Ordway later thought it was the volunteer fire chief from Quiktupac, John Scratching Water, lines of black and white ash all over his face, the father, a lot of people had said, of twenty-five children.

"I'm a poet," was all Ordway could think to respond, although it didn't feel at all odd.

"A poet?" John Scratching Water said. He looked around immediately to see if the television van was near. It was not.

"Yes, I am," Ordway said.

John Scratching Water turned toward his truck then and the three men standing there and said, "He's a poet."

One of the Quiktupac men walked over to the truck from St. A de P and said something there, although by this time a few of the spectators had also picked it up and were whispering among themselves.

THEY ALL, HOWEVER, HEARD the scream, a thin wail from the top of the steeple, Fantasia Johnson not only alone but also able to look down and see the blazing hole that was now the church, the arrogant torch that the wood and brick steeple was becoming, and maybe even the end of any life she might hope to have.

Nothing could be done.

JOHN SCRATCHING WATER COULD see that. He pulled his eyes away from Fantasia and settled on Ordway for just a moment. He smiled with dirty tears rolling down his cheeks and finally said to Ordway, "I see."

He walked an enlarging circle around Ordway then, whispering out of the fire noise, "He's a poet," as people backed slowly away, clearing, in just a few minutes, a circle around Ordway fifty feet across, Ordway alone against that furious mockery even as John Scratching Water tried to calm the anguish of the crowd with a simple "That's all that can be done now."

Life

ILLUSIONS

The coal room was off in the corner of the cellar, just beyond the old furnace and the stoker unit. Although the furnace hadn't been used in years, there was still about a half ton of coal left in the room, itself about six-foot square and walled on two sides by walls of four-by-four lumber. It was smelly and chemically suspect. Jim had decided long ago that the air in the room was undoubtedly filled with the molecules of unfriendly substances, both from the coal itself and from the oils that had seeped into the wood and concrete over the years.

He was not about to haul the coal away, however, and with the furnace permanently disconnected from the old chimney there was no longer any question of burning it. He would have done neither anyway, since he had a need to go down there periodically, take off all his clothes, and wiggle himself a seat into the pile and sit. With the walls and enough of the coal piled up around him he could find an almost soundless solitude and that was good, that was the need—or one of them. Sometimes he would masturbate while he was down there and that was a need, too, but that didn't happen too often. The sitting and the nakedness were not sexual things; it was only that the time down there was an uncommitted time and occasionally he would make that his commitment.

More often than not he wondered if the coal residue, always hard to wash out, particularly on his back and the backs of his legs, would someday give him skin cancer. Once in a while he would slither himself so deeply into the pile that he would be completely covered except for his head. Emerging, he would be a greasy black. The very first time he'd done that he'd had to put gray duct tape on the bottoms of his feet just so that he could make his way to the shower on the second floor without causing permanent stains on either the carpeting or the hardwood floors. After that he always came down with a pair of old sneakers. The shower, too, usually took a full can of Comet to clean, and once he got the routine systematized, he would precede it by buying a packet of washcloths at a discount store: two for him and one for the shower, all to be thrown away.

The house itself had been built by his grandfather. Cedar-shake siding, durable in the stiff Quilli winters, dormers in front. "Just an adorable little Cape," he often told people. He had inherited the house when his father died the year following his mother's death. Jim had been living in an apartment on the edge of the ratty Hunellia Faulk Ponus Park. No coal room there, of course, but he'd had thick carpeting, the elephant collection from his mother, good quality knickknacks, and the thirty or so original oil paintings that he'd picked up over the years at the Bangor and Fryeburg fairs and craft gatherings in Quilli. He had no illusions that he was harboring emerging greatness, but they were real works generated from a real artistic impulse, no matter how primitive or unrealized the potential, and their presence on his walls could snatch him away from boredom or depression or just the general disgust with living that he occasionally felt as quickly as you might want. They made him see things differently during times when he didn't like what he was seeing at all. Beyond that, they looked good and had made his tiny place feel comfortable and well tended.

He had thought about selling the house and investing the money. Since there were still a good twenty years to go before his retirement, that investment, along with his teacher's pension, would have allowed him to forget about the problem of retirement, about the endless cycle of accumulation and preparation for infirmity. It would be done, complete. He would be of means and could do things. But he would not sell the house.

He had neighbors on one side, an old couple, and a field on the other and a view sliding down the low horizon into New Brunswick. It truly seemed to Jim that everyone was an old couple these days except him. As far as he could tell, the woman was blind and badly stooped over, almost shrunken it seemed, whereas the man was surely the opposite: quite tall, well over two hundred pounds, and apparently as fit and able as he had probably ever been. Jim liked to think there was something of a doting relationship between them—he just wanted to believe that, he later decided—but he had never seen them out together without also seeing a look of deep disgust and deep impatience on the man's face. Once they had been out walking—Jim had seen this while sitting on his front steps—and the man, responding to things of which Jim could only guess, had reached down and wrapped the old woman around the waist with his arm and carried her the final twenty or thirty feet into the house.

Life had been good to Jim and he had returned the compliment with a modest contentment. He was uncommonly good in the classroom—he taught speech to eighth graders—good enough to have been nominated more times than he cared to remember for Teacher of the Year. Yet if that excellence inspired jealousy among his lesser colleagues, the jealousy was mitigated by Jim's never having actually won the award. There was always an older teacher who managed to squeeze him out with the sympathy vote, or some younger, untenured one whose ha-ha ways inspired that honorific welcome into the profession. Honor, indeed, Jim scoffed. Within a year the youngster was usually on the way to a new position at some other, more prestigious school. There was an irony to the business that Jim appreciated, but no sense of loss since he could imagine no particular purpose or end that the honor could serve in his life.

HE HAD ANCHORED THE stepladder to his work-bench with two-by-fours. The thing had to take a lot of strain and if it ever fell over—and, God forbid, out of reach—while he was hanging from the ankle cuffs he would have been in a strait. He could imagine how the tendons around his ankles would slowly pull away from his feet as too many hours passed, could imagine his stomach muscles virtually shredding as he tried some sort of inverted sit-up to reach one of the joists above, then to—what? Calmly uncuff himself to fall right down onto those shattered joints? That would hurt, as would the dragging journey up the stairs somehow to dress and call an ambulance.

One day, he was out washing windows on the driveway side of the house when his neighbor stepped outside and sat down on a bench on his rear porch. He knew the man was staring at him, but with Windex in hand, Jim just kept on working. Jim's smile had always been ready to expand into a hello and even a conversation, but the old man had never done more than nod his head and that but barely. When Jim finished his work and went inside he glanced through his dining room window and noticed that the man was no longer there.

The second time it happened Jim was waxing his car and the man brought out a folding chair of plastic webbing and sat in his yard watching him. Jim didn't know what to do. At least this was no series of covert looks or sideways glances. The man was flat-out staring at him the way—so Jim thought—only someone who was very close to you would do while not feeling obligated to help you with your work, or who was close enough to know that waxing a car was a personal thing and that you did not want anyone's help. Jim often felt that way about onerous tasks.

LIVING ALONE HAD ALWAYS made it easy for Jim to satisfy whatever whim for luxury he might have. If he wanted a big steak or a fresh lobster from the tank at Don's Grocery he could have that. If he wanted to go on a trip he could do it. If he wanted to order some expensive weirdness that was tucked into his American Express bill or that fell out of the Sunday *Boston Globe* as an irresistible insert, well, he could, and occasionally did, order such things. Mostly, though, if he had a need for elegance, he would simply put on his mother's old fur coat and the pair of heels he'd bought from a catalog. He had no idea what kind of fur the coat was. It was old, of course, with patches beginning to show where the fur was falling out. Mostly, it seemed to be black, although it could glow itself into a deep and rich auburn if he held it at the right angle in the sun. Black bear, he joked with himself, or black squirrel. In any case, it was incredibly soft and warm, and he often wished he could wear it outside in the winter.

Jim glanced out one of his upstairs windows and noticed his neighbor's old Dodge sitting there wet in the old man's driveway, the green garden hose snaking through the grass to one of the basement windows and then down through it. Later, while he was sitting under his apple tree reading a book, he saw the man come out and cover the car with paste wax. Jim didn't think it was smart to cover the whole thing with wax first and then begin to wipe it off—stuff would dry on there like a zipper suit—but he didn't think it was his place to instruct the old guy.

Eventually, the man came out onto the back porch, one hand cupping his wife's elbow as they went down the stairs and through the grass to the car. She had a big white rag in each hand and before long she was bent over the car and rubbing away at the white paste, wisps of wiry gray hair dangling over her cheeks and ears, a sheen of sweat on her face and neck. The man sat in the webbed chair while she worked and occasionally would get up to direct one of her hands over to some spot that she had missed. There was irritation in his face as he did so, but the old woman just smiled and nodded her head and said, "Okay, Okay."

ONE DAY, JIM DID have a conversation with the old man that was remarkable in its detail and finality.

"How long have you been married?" Jim asked.

"Five hundred years," the old man said.

"Seems like, huh?" Jim said, smiling.

"If you say so."

"What's her name?"

"Dolly."

"Dolly?"

"Yup."

She had been hitchhiking, the old man said, and he'd picked her up, amazed and amused by her audacity and hooked by her beauty. He'd also been shocked that anyone that slim and that pretty would be lacking for transport. "I was loose then and quite young," he said, "and foolish to the point of nearly shaking that

I'd actually stopped and picked her up. I had done that before, you see, but they were usually just roust-abouts you could abandon any place you felt like, knowing they were just grateful for any mileage you gave them—or you could take them out somewhere and pound the crap out of them and even bugger them just because that was the mood you were in at the time. This, however—her, she—was different and I couldn't handle it. She was as bouncy as an old car spring and talked and talked and talked until finally I just took her out to what must have been the back road of a back road up near St. A de P and had such way as I pleased. A youthful mistake, you might say. But it set in motion a lot of things until I finally thought, if she can't identify me, that will be the end of it, so I got an ice pick from the glove box and gouged out the brown parts of her eyes after stuffing an old rag in her mouth because I figured she'd scream, not that there was anybody to hear. Then I saw her squirming around in pain with blood all over her face and I thought there will be hell to pay and ret-ribution and, you know, son, I just thought, Well, let's let it to hell begin here. I was going to kill her just to put her out of her misery and to cover my tracks, but an amazing force in me flipped me into a different direction and I decided that it was now up to me to care for her the rest of both our days. Can you imagine such a thing? I mean I was judge and jury and I sentenced me to providing for her and that was that. We been together now all our lives and we done all right, as you can see."

Jim looked over at the woman. She was now on her knees and feeling her way with her rags over the front bumper of the car. She seemed to have that look of anybody who's working very hard at something and gaining some kind of satisfaction from the work.

JIM SET THE U-HAUL box of his school things down on the kitchen table and stood for a moment and basked in the sweet realization that the school year was finally over. Good to begin, good to end, a sweet and zesty cycle really.

He did feel that there was truly nothing left inside his head, that his mind had turned into Styrofoam package stuffers, mood beans. A light breeze past his ears could rattle them all around in a dry flutter.

. . .

ONE SUNDAY AFTERNOON JIM went for a drive in his new car. He had timed the purchase so he could enjoy its newness over the course of the summer. Eventually he pulled off the road, a pond right there and not far from where the old Indian lived in a trailer with some young woman—so he'd heard—one of them blind; he'd heard that, too. He hoped it wasn't the woman who was blind. Jim felt uneasy even thinking about blind women—let alone having one for a neighbor.

It was a favorite spot and most of the time he would be the only one there, free to push his way through the heavy brush beneath the tall maples and pine trees in the place, free to wander barefoot or even to take off all his clothes and get scratched up a bit, pausing near the water to do some exercises, sweating, or even scaring the shit out of himself when he would hear a car pull off the road near his own car and he would have to scramble for his clothes. He often thought of these acts as calls that he was answering, quite fundamental rebellions having something to do with urban growth or the destruction of solitude or just the imposition of too many restrictions designed to make life orderly or at least to keep the traffic moving. He never analyzed these moves to any great degree, finding it adequate simply to note the string lying on the ground once in a while and to follow it out for as long as his interests held.

The old Dodge was parked in Jim's usual spot and Jim found that to be quite a coincidence, enough that he considered driving on and going elsewhere to avoid the embarrassment of anyone thinking that anyone was following anyone else around. On the other hand —Jim liked it when his rebel self stood up and demanded an accounting like some doughty old adjutant—let people think what they wanted to think.

They were down where the stream ran into the pond and she was standing in the water naked, her lumpy butt just hanging there beneath the predictable rolls of fat at her waist and up under her arms. The old man was next to her with a bucket that he was dipping into the stream and emptying over her head. The stream was moving fast and Jim thought the water looked cold. He could hear the sounds of their voices, but he was not close enough to hear any words. The tone seemed light and he thought he heard a laugh now and again. Once, she backhanded him into his belly and he let out a mock "oof" and emptied another bucket over her. She seemed to sense then that he was still fully clothed and reached up and started unbuttoning his shirt. He backed away a step and she persisted until finally he pushed her hard on her chest and she sat down with a splash in the water. He raised his face skyward then and let out a roar of laughter that the woman did not share, staring blankly toward the other side of the stream. Finally, she raised her left arm up out of the water and toward him. The man shook his head and Jim thought he could hear him say "Oh no," but the woman kept her arm up, her fingers wiggling impatiently at him, gesturing, a kind of "come here" that he seemed to be resisting.

He took her hand and right away Jim could see the knot of muscles in her arm tightening up, could see the old man slowly twisting around, bending at one knee, a look of great anger and great panic on his face as he bent toward the water, the woman laughing now, her one arm seeming to wrap itself up into the very fiber of the man while the fingers of her other hand seemed to be just lightly tapping or skimming the surface of the water, a relaxed gesture, something so natural in the shady sun with the water dancing and the tree branches fluttering around that

232

Jim could imagine an artist or photographer bearing down on that hand, framing it, giving it thought and frozen beauty.

He walked away then, hearing a loud splash a few moments later. For a moment he had an image in his mind of the two of them walking toward the front door of their house, her arm around *his* waist and carrying him up the steps.

The next night, as they were returning from their walk, a car drove past them, honked once, and then pulled into their driveway. A woman got out, very tall —Jim saw her from his front porch—wearing heels and jeans and some sort of combination of shirt and blouse, something casual yet in a definite style from somewhere.

In the morning—Jim usually got up around four during the summer—he noticed that the lights were on in the house next door and that the woman's car was still in the driveway. Wearing only a pair of cut-offs, he started out toward his garage to get his garbage can to haul out to the front when he saw her sitting there in the webbed chair. Between the full moon and a splash of streetlight coming up his drive-way, they could see each other fairly well. She had a can of something—he couldn't tell if it was soda or beer—in her hand and she was smoking a cigarette.

"Good morning," she said as Jim walked by carrying the big plastic can.

"Hello," he said. "Nice out, isn't it? This time of day?"

"Always," she answered. "Real nice. Are you Jim?"

"Yes."

"Nice to meet you, Jim. Steve told me your name."

"Steve."

"Dolly's husband. I'm sorry—I guess he did tell me you've all never really met."

"Not actually, I suppose. We talked once. A few words over the garden hose. We didn't get around to names. Way neighbors are sometimes. Not much to it."

"Sure. A lot of distance, isn't there? Always."

Jim wondered if she could see the coal oil stains on his body. There was at least ten or fifteen feet of space separating them and he knew that from where she sat he would have the dark sky at his back. As he continued on down, he would pass into the streetlight for a moment. If she turned around to watch him walk down—well, you saw what you saw. His heart and all the other guys were tamed for a time.

"Sometimes not enough," he said.

As he walked on he turned that comment over in his mind and regretted it. He'd just meant for it to be the equivalent of a philosophical sigh, but it could easily have sounded egregiously snotty.

Hasty comments. Damn, Sam—not even buttons or a Band-Aid.

He walked quickly, the stones in his gravel drive cushioned by the tape on his feet. He put the can down on the grass at the edge of the street and crossed over the front of his house to go down the walkway on the other side to the back door. He would try a good shower and get himself cleaned up and dressed and if she was still there then maybe a little coffee, certainly more civility on his part—even an apology.

"Hello again," she said, standing by his back door.

"Shit!"

"I'm sorry! God, I must have scared the hell out of you. I'm really sorry!"

In the light from his kitchen she could see him, or at least enough of him to make him feel like folding his arms across his chest or sitting down on the steps and curling himself into a ball. Jim wouldn't do that, however, not standing by his own back door.

"It's all right," he said quietly.

"You followed them around," she said. "Out by the pond. Why was that?"

"It wasn't. I mean, there wasn't any 'why' to it. It just happened. I didn't know they—he, excuse me—saw me, though."

"He didn't."

"Oh?"

"I did."

"Right. Well—listen, I've been, uh, doing some work. I need a shower so—"

"I can see that."

"If I'm not quite as sociable as I might—"

"She's dying. That's the thing."

Maybe forty-five, Jim thought. A look of having been around, whatever that was. Eyes barely seen in the dawn, a certain distance or a certain unbending over facts. Lies, he told his students, stick to the wrinkles of your eyes and make them get bigger. Nice story. He wondered if they could cause your ankles to swell, too. "Who's dying?" he asked. "The old woman? Is she your mother?"

"Oh, no. She's not my mother."

"Seems fairly old, though. I suppose it's time."

"It's time?"

"I know. Didn't sound right even as I said it. Must be the hour. It's not a sensitive time of day."

"I'll see you later, Jim."

"Sure," he said.

HE TRIED THE MAKEUP that night, the familiar urge quite there but seeming to struggle up against a clot of something inside, some feeling of misdirection or confusion, a clouding of purpose or a watering down of what was usually a jittery nervousness of clear intent. This is my own time, he'd thought, and I answer to me. What I want is what I want. Clearly angry with himself, and knowing there was nothing on television worth watching that night, he'd gotten his big jar of cold cream and cleaned it all off. It was nearly eight o'clock anyway, about time for bed.

Jim went outside then and walked around the yard thinking out a list of yard things he might do the next day. The grass, of course. He'd only cut it about a week ago, but at this time of year you could do it nearly anytime and make a difference. He had some wild plum trees that badly needed cutting and shaping and he'd been putting that off for over a year. The sharp spines made working on them difficult, and the way the branches wove into and around themselves—well, it was a scratchy chore, a lot of sweat and some random blood.

He'd been wanting to paint the old garage for a long time, too, but as he walked out to it he was hit by the same indecision that always popped up. It was time to tear it down and either build a new one or have the greasy dirt plowed deep and planted into lawn. Since he traded his cars every three years the way his father had always done, it wasn't as though he needed the shelter to preserve the timeless zing of whatever machine he happened to be driving.

They were sitting there as he walked past and Jim nodded politely. The old man—Steve?—was sitting in the chair. He was wearing a pair of shorts and a T shirt with what looked like some kind of garish design on it, his legs crossed at the knee. He was also wearing sunglasses, which Jim thought was odd in the twilight, but he also thought it was odd that the younger woman was standing by him holding what looked like a small tape recorder with the sounds of a baseball game coming out of it.

• • •

FUNERAL THINGS WERE GOING on next door. Jim could tell that, though he knew he could not have cited any evidence. He supposed the old woman had died and he felt bad about that.

The shades of their house were no longer drawn on his side as they had been earlier and he wished he'd taken a walk to see if they'd been drawn all over the house. He had assumed it was he they were shutting out, but he hadn't known that for sure.

As he returned from Don's Grocery he saw a van parked in their driveway. Later, two men wheeled a cart out with a body on it, but it was all covered up and Jim's angle was bad so he couldn't tell who it was. He checked the obituaries for the next couple of days. Since he didn't know their last name he looked for a Steve or Steven or Stephen or Dolores or Dolly but nothing came up. There had always been a lot of name changing in town, though—even Jim wasn't sure if he remembered how to spell the original of his own last name—so he wasn't surprised, and none of the street addresses of the recently deceased even came close. Sometimes all you got was a line or two and not even your address.

From the attic he could see into their yard. She was

wearing, he thought, a quite extraordinarily skimpy swimsuit. The bottom was cut such that, well, her bottom was simply there, holdable rounds, cheese maybe or possibly ham.

She was shaving Steve, holding a bowl of water in her hand while he sat there with his chin upraised and a towel around his neck, wearing the sunglasses in the twilight, the tape recorder sitting there on the grass.

Jim went back down to the first floor, stopping in his bedroom first to get the bottle of nail polish. He'd gone from the kitchen to the attic, lifted around ten or twelve heavy boxes, and back downstairs again and he thought his heart rate was a languid sixty, maybe sixty-five. The walking was responsible for that, another summer ritual. Each morning at exactly nine he left the house, walked two miles out into the country, and then back in only minutes over an hour. Anyone watching could see that Jim was serious about his walking, although from his point of view it was truly a relaxing time. His mind trembled and skimmed over anything and everything: nonsense, gibberish, serious thought, planning, and much, much reflection. He would sigh deeply over injustices that had been done to him, hold long and rather sprightly conversations with God ("Well, God, I don't know—"), quick partnership chats, plan his meals or budget a purchase, or ruminate with a hard logic and cunning over his imaginary falcon, Glory.

Glory came alive during those walks but never at any other time. This was, routinely genteel or not, exercise, a time for the body to endure halters and traces and for the mind, concomitantly, to be given some unfettered time off. Allowed to wander, it sometimes roared and sometimes whimpered, had seen a crow one day reflected in the water as Jim crossed over Wulustuk Stream, and had brought Glory out of that. Glory was good, a high flyer that gave Jim an aerial view of life and its drudgeries or life and its joys. He knew nothing of falconry except some dross that he had picked up in his reading over the years. But there was a time—most days, but not all of them, when he would be in the dip and curve just beyond the creek, a point where the homes had stopped but the nasty loneliness of boundless forest had not yet begun, where no one could see him—when, if he felt like it, he would slowly raise his right arm upward, feeling the thick leather cuff going from wrist to elbow, the gesture almost liturgical, clearly a calling forth, and with a slow fart, an uninhibited belch, or a simple "Yo, bub," she would be there, hooded, alert, and anxious, black, sleek, and mean as hell. Unhooded, she would dig her talons into the cuff before she made that quick, flapping leap into the sky, the soaring an end point following such lecturing as Jim might have had need of that day.

IT WAS TOO LATE to get into anything that evening. In the morning he would do some selecting, work out a plan for the month. He was quite methodical in his studying because he knew the work would be boring. He would give himself a half hour each day for a play, fifteen minutes for the poems, and then another hour for methods. He'd take a final hour then for the texts and that would be that. It was what teachers were expected to do during the summer and he did it. Besides, three hours a day could be endured under any umbrella, especially since he knew that at the end of the month he would be different. There would be an awareness and there would be thoughts that had never been there before, images of people who had been images themselves, hybrids, collections of colors and virtues and weaknesses, physical anomalies: scar tissue and great marshmallow breasts, the limbless poor or a noseless king, the touchingly barren and the striated fruitful—dragons and pissheads and rogues and assholes and somewhere in all that the boundlessly good who always seem to find themselves with babies ripped screaming from gashed bellies or red-hot pincers applied to the balls.

"Hello there," he said to Steve and the woman, feeling composed and good over the organization he'd just imposed on his life. There was a television tray table in front of Steve and he was eating from a plate of fiddleheads and bacon and eggs and toast. A cup of coffee and a glass of orange juice were beside the plate.

The woman looked at him and said, "Hello, Jim. How are you tonight?"

"Doing fine," he said. He noticed then that the tape recorder was playing a newscast, having that kind of hollow or echoey sound of having been taken from a TV.

"Your house looks nice, Jim," she said. "You do work at it, don't you?"

"Not as much as I might, I guess. But I try to keep it up. Sure. Thanks."

"Don't mention it. You deserve it."

For a moment she seemed either dissatisfied with or uncomfortable in the swimsuit. She bent over, her shoulders hunched, the straps falling toward her elbows. As her breasts came out, she tugged at the fabric, pulling it and smoothing it, hooking her fingers under the cloth at the bottom and pulling at that. She stopped then, seeming, as Jim saw it, not to feel at all self-conscious about either him or Steve, quite tenderly taking both breasts in her hands as though she were somehow going to adjust those too, looking down at herself. Finally, taking a deep breath and exhaling slowly, she pulled the suit back up and adjusted the straps on her shoulders.

Jim hadn't pretended not to watch, although Steve had just kept on eating. Once during the ritual she looked up at Jim and smiled and he'd smiled back. It was at that moment, however, that the tape recorder intruded and he'd recognized the voice of the vice president of the television station. It was the daily editorial and Jim remembered hearing it already that day and recalled that the editorial was done only during the first two newscasts of the day.

"Steve?" Jim said.

"Um?"

"I just wanted to tell you—I mean, I came over, I haven't had a chance to say anything about your wife. So. Naturally, you have my sympathies—if there's anything I can do—"

Jim could see a dribble of egg on Steve's stubbly chin as the man looked up at him, a forkful of egg and fiddleheads poised for a moment on the way to his mouth. "Who the hell are you?" he asked.

JIM'S WALK THE NEXT day was a good one, the sky clear and a light wind lifting his sweat away. The stream was running at a full bubble and he stopped to look down at it just after releasing Glory for her hunt. The water was brown and stirred up and the bubbles reflected dully in the early light. He looked up once and could see her just hanging there, stationary and balanced in the wind stream, the cold and unfriendly eyes either finding him familiar or at least concluding that he was too big to tear into. He looked around to make sure no cars were coming—one, maybe two per walk were the most that ever came by and most days he had his route completely to himself—and then peed through the bridge railing.

Steve was in trouble.

Indeed he was. What followed from that, however, seemed to be nothing at all. The man was at least seventy. How could you be in trouble at that age?

The innocent smile, a blend, Jim thought, of maturity and sass. Jim had looked out of his bedroom window just once before going to sleep the night before. They were still there. Steve was still in the chair. She was sitting on the grass in front of him, the whiteness of one arm looking like it was draped across the lower part of her abdomen, the hand either in a deeper shadow or else tucked into the crotch of the swimsuit. He had been tempted to set his alarm for 2 A.M. just to check, but he decided not to do that. Of course they'd be there. Of course she'd be serving Steve lunch right in the middle of the night.

He heard Glory before he saw her, that slight disturbance, that tilting in the angle of the wind. She didn't touch a damn thing, but it sounded like her wingtips just barely brushing the leaves as she swooped the airspace over the creek, coming toward Jim like a fuzzy bullet just inches from his head and passing by, on down the stream to where it curved away by a small broccoli field and then into the field in a tumbling flutter of wings and dust, climbing in a moment back into the air with something dangling from her beak, her wings working hard until she hit some moving air and began to climb.

JIM WAS HANGING BY his ankle cuffs when she walked in on him. He was wearing the high heels and a jockstrap, his body covered with the oily coal dust, when he first heard her: the outside door to the basement opening, a light and squeaky groaning to the half-dozen wooden steps, a presence then, a change in temperature to the musty air. For an instant, there was a surge of all the protective devices, the muscle tension, the adrenal squirt, even the laughingly bizarre start—and end—of a hard-on. Then it all passed as he thought, This is whatever it is. Welcome to my home, whoever you are.

"Jim?"

He thought it should be pretty obvious. "Yes?"

"Steve's asleep."

"Oh."

"He's taking a nap."

"That's nice, you know. That's nice."

"Old guys like that. Are you in any pain?"

There was an old wooden box near the furnace that

she pulled over near him. She sat down. Jim's father had liked that box. It had come over from Poland long enough ago to be perhaps an antique. Their address had been burned into it and there was still some kind of postage mark painted on it near the address.

"No," he said. "It's more of a—pressure. A whole general kind of pressure."

"Before, too?"

"Oh, yes."

"And after?"

"You have nice knees," Jim said. "I like your knees."

Jim's arms were hanging with the fingertips barely off of the concrete floor. She reached down and took his hand and brought it up to one knee. He caressed it lightly, then squeezed it, pressing his fingers around the kneecap and along the sides of the joint. He brought his arm down finally, noticing that her knee was now smudged from his dirty hand.

"You didn't know them at all, did you?" she asked.

"Steve and Dolly?"

"Steve and Dolly."

"Not at all. I guess I assumed they were friends of my parents over the years. I tried, but she was always with him and was never, well . . . and he, I don't know. It doesn't matter, though."

"They were rough people, Jim. Very rough."

"Why don't you give me a hand here?"

"Are you done?"

"Yes."

SHE BEGAN COMING OVER each day at seven in the morning and they became lovers, although she always left right at nine when Jim took his walk. Several times he invited her along, but each time she refused, saying only that it was time for her to get back over there and go to bed. He didn't mind that because he'd never shared Glory with anyone and wasn't sure how he would do that had the woman ever actually come along. Most days they made love twice, but since some of the time was used either to get him down if he was hanging or get him cleaned off if he'd been in the coal, there was never enough time to clear away the passion, to indulge in some idle talk, creamy whispers of the past, or childhoods gone or adult dreams lost, found, or otherwise provided for. He did want her to come along, but she wouldn't and he regretted that.

They could talk out there and he knew she wouldn't say a thing about Glory. He knew that. Well, she might ask some things, but they would be the right things: How old is she? What is her wingspan? Does a bird like that live all alone?

HE BEGAN INTERRUPTING HIS sleep in order to watch them, knowing that in the stillness she could hear his alarm clock go off at midnight and that she knew, too, that he was watching them. Most nights she would at some point—he thought she was trying to guess his movements—walk back to the house and turn on the porch light. It couldn't have been much more than a forty-watt bulb, but it was enough so that from where he sat in the darkness of his back porch he could see them clearly. Steve always had the sunglasses on and she'd added a baseball cap to his wardrobe, which he seemed to wear whenever the tape recorder was giving forth a ballgame, always the Red Sox. One night—he wasn't sure if she was doing this just for him or not—she stood about ten feet from Steve with a baseball bat in her hands. She was naked, of course; in fact Jim thought that with the exception of the early evening when it was still fairly light, she seemed to be naked nearly all the time. In the morning, certainly, when she scooted self-consciously between their houses —both coming to his and going back (he had offered her one of his shirts the first time, but she had refused, grinning at him and shaking her head)—and somehow he couldn't imagine that she went back to the house and put on some kind of granny gown before going to sleep; and then at night, every night. Well— lucky Steve, he thought. Lucky Jim?

The one night, though, she stood back from Steve, taking practice swings with the bat, looking as though she were coordinating her movements with something on the tape recorder, holding the bat in a nicely balanced and slightly choked grip, moving several steps toward the older man finally until she seemed to be lining up her swing quite level with the back of Steve's head. A roar seemed to echo over from the machine as she arced the bat in a powerful swing and then looked up, smiling, into the stands over Jim's porch, releasing the bat and trotting over to Jim's porch, looking at him and raising her fingers up in a double V, then loping out and over to his crab apple tree, his old garage, and then back just to the left of Steve where she turned, arms upraised, in a full circle.

Jim would rise at midnight and sit out there and watch them for several hours—watch her, actually, since Steve just sat in his chair the whole time—and then go in at around four or five, nap briefly, have some breakfast, go down to the coal room or spend some time in his bathroom if he was in the mood for that run of things—a lot messier but certainly not as dirty—and then wait for her to come over.

SHE FINALLY HIT STEVE squarely in the back of the head with the baseball bat and Jim decided he'd known all along that that was going to happen. First, Glory had been giving out—signals? Twice now in the days before it happened she left his arm, spiraled upward in a crazy flight until she hit a breeze or wind current, then after catching it she seemed suddenly to fold her wings inward, dropping quickly, letting herself plummet nearly into the stream before taking flight—but then only back to his arm. She didn't hunt and she didn't kill. Her head seemed to droop with or without her hood on and she didn't fight the hooding. All of that was unusual. He thought it must be a parasite or a virus—perhaps a drop or two of mineral oil in her feed would do something.

Then there was the woman herself. For as playful as she had begun to be in the evening—her game had become more complex since she had started stealing bases, sliding into second or third with a breast-bouncing jolt up against the crab-apple tree or the loose boards of the garage, arguing with an unseen umpire, standing there trying to brush grass stains or greasy garage dirt off of her thigh or calf—the mornings seemed no longer a friendly time for their private amusements. She might be above him with the early sun reflecting off her hair, the air light, the house itself seeming to be sweeping out the remnants of the previous day's heat, and she would stop, her head turning toward the window, her muscles tensing up not only on him and not just the tenseness of stress or an uneasy thought. They seemed to knot up and mound and curve like those of a power lifter, her belly rippling, her head slowly tilting back, and even her breasts almost disappearing under a cording of chest muscle. They were under no illusions of either love or even the most remote affection—Jim still didn't know her name—but at those moments he felt himself to be more of a biological observer than a lover. His bed was a specimen tray and unseen agents had apparently dosed her with powerful experimental liquors or had upped the voltage on an electrode. More and more she seemed this large, twisting, writhing column of proteins, a slight, gaspy moan her only sound, something there within and genuinely frightening going all singular of purpose. They were connected and he could feel her tightness, but he could also feel as though he were just some sort of platform. He wanted to make her talk and at least begin to voice an exchange of endearments, to smile maybe so that one of them could say, "I really like this," and the other could agree, with a breathless chuckle that they could both continue then into a quiet laugh. The tender words wouldn't have to be silly. They could even be —it really would fit—factual: the two of them just mouthing adjustments, a shift here, a molding of the flesh over there and here let me get you a glass of water. Do you vote in elections? I don't have to suck your breasts if you don't like it. Why have you reversed Steve's days and I wonder if this mole is precancerous. You should at least cover it when you sit in the coal. Nobody knows about coal oil. No one ever has. I like it when you wear my shoes. I like it just before the game is rained out, the joy and chatter of the crowd so muffled and almost cozy under the rolling wadding of fierce clouds, clouds of lavender and incipient fire, voices pushing down into themselves as the first drops fall with runners left on base, exposed, waiting, mercilessly held out there at the umpire's discretion, wondering how it feels to be right there between the sky and the earth when the lightning strikes—two out and a man (woman) on. Wait, I have to sneeze. It's all right. Well, I can't sneeze with your toes in my mouth. Is Steve asleep? Steve's dead. No, he's not. Oh. I thought he was.

She wouldn't talk, though, at least not quietly in whispers and sighs. When she spoke she sounded like she was chairing a difficult meeting or ordering unusual food in an expensive restaurant.

"Of course, Jim. I understand. We'll look into it."

So, he thought, I stand at third base and coach, calculating tendencies and distances, whims and will and a whole catalog of fantasies at risk.

"If you like. Certainly. There is no reason why we cannot."

DESTINY WAS CERTAINLY DIFFERENT from planning. As she loped by him this time, somewhat dotted and speckled with the backsplash of blood and bits of jellied brain tissue—Jim himself caught off guard and sitting there with a hot dog he'd just pulled from the micro—she smiled at him and seemed to mouth "Check him out, Jim," but Jim could only sit for a time, struck by his own lack of surprise and lack of shock and lack of any need to bolt over his porch railing and run to the convulsing lump of clothing lying there on the ground.

Destiny was never planned, he thought. You either had it in you or you didn't.

LATER, AS HE WAS hanging in his basement and waiting for her to come over, he wondered how Glory would be that day. Just fine, he thought. He knew that. Probably all along it had been nothing more than simple jealousy, a one-thought, primitive perception that she had lost his complete attention. Today she would fly and she would hunt, and Jim could continue his reveries of putting people into the houses as he passed by, giving them activities and purposes, livening up the dull and unpopulated yards and porches and gardens, putting cars out there that were ready to go somewhere and displacing the constant run of delivery vans and repair trucks. Once, he had seen a chimney sweep working up on a roof and that singular human presence had been almost like a revelation. But it had, indeed, been singular. No one lived in these houses, or at least they didn't live in them the way he lived in his: shaped by the dwelling in what he was and what he did.

The stairs squeaked the way they usually did when she came over, the only difference this time being the sliding thump as she pulled Steve after her, releasing it in a heap as she stepped through the door into the basement. It had begun to stiffen up after the accident, with one arm sticking straight out and the other—well. Hanging upside down was not the best way to sort out the objectivity of a thing, but it looked as though the wrist was kind of across Steve's face with the thumb of that hand caught in his eye socket, the fingers sticking straight up. Jim wrung his hands together and sighed deeply as she came over and stood near him. She had not washed, and although Jim could have blamed the body, he knew that the fresh stink in the room came from her. It is, he thought, like earth gone bad.

"Why did you bring the body?" he asked.

"I couldn't just leave it there, Jim. It's light out now. What would the neighbors think?"

I am the neighbors, thought Jim.

"An accident. A game. I saw you play it every night. A stupid thing, maybe, to look back on. But he enjoyed it. I know he did. He was old but he wasn't dead and all the prancing around you did—he enjoyed that, until you got too close."

"Prancing? Jesus."

"You tell them that. It's all so crazy that I don't think anyone could believe anything other than what you tell them."

She squatted down on the floor near his head then, her hand coming up to his face and gently brushing against the stubble of his morning whiskers. "I'm glad you've been here," she said.

She studied Steve's body for a moment and then worked quickly. She slid the big wooden box over near it and lifted Steve by the shoulders and dumped him in. The one arm with the hand stuck in the eye went in first and that was all right, although the other stuck straight up out of the container. She got a hammer and nail then and, with what Jim could see was a lot of effort, bent it down inside and nailed it through the palm to the inside of the box. It worked pretty much the same with the lower part of the body. Both knees were bent—he'd fallen out of the chair that way—but where one leg was bent right up to his chest the other was straighter. She had to straddle it and the box to weight it down so she could put a nail through the foot. Jim thought it was odd that she didn't even take the old man's sandal off but nailed right through it.

"HE'S IN YOUR GARAGE," she said. She was breathing heavily, her body streaked with dirt and gore. She saw the puddle below Jim and the stream running toward the floor drain and said, "I'm sorry. Please don't be embarrassed."

"I won't be," Jim said. "Why don't you give me a hand here?"

He didn't realize the strength that lay behind that knotty frieze of muscle she displayed for him each morning. It reminded him of one of those body-building contests, with all of that artful strutting and gassy contorting. It had never occurred to him that there was a substance beyond the show, but of course there was and she handled him easily in getting the pressure off the ankles and in undoing the cuffs.

"Now what?" he asked, curious as to what she might want to do next, thinking for a moment of how sometimes Glory—at the moment when he removed the hood—would turn her head enough so that he knew she was looking at him, that single-eyed and sideways stare always chilling. "You are the word *hawk*," he said one time, "a short and scary word." He popped his lips then and at the burst of air she jerked her head and flew off. "Don't forget," he shouted, "with the change of one gene you'd be a chicken."

"What do you mean, Jim?"

"It wasn't an accident, was it? I mean, you didn't just happen to get too caught up in the spirit of the game and move a shade too close."

"Did you know she took his eyes?"

"Who?"

"Dolly. A short time before she died she took them. As deeds go, it was complicated enough, but she took them. Retired to her room for over a day. I think she ate them but I don't know that. That's too disgusting for me, I can tell you—Jim."

"The sunglasses—"

"He was hardly concerned about his image."

"He never saw you?"

"Only you did, Jim."

As a final step, when all the hauling had been done, Jim hired a company to come in and take out about two feet of the surface soil. Then a garden company came with a load of fresh topsoil. They just dumped it so he went out himself with a rake and shovel and smoothed it all out. Even with his walking around on it it was still about a foot above the surface of the rest of the yard. The settling out should be good, he knew, and hoped for a few days of rain soon since that would speed the process along.

Eventually, he thought, he'd have the whole driveway dug up and planted over. He could park his car on the street just like most of his neighbors and it would even make it easier for people to tell when he was home—except, perhaps, when he was out on his walks, but none of them were home at that time anyway. As courtesies go, it was right up there with leaving your porch light on all night. A little something—not much.

GLORY

Elsie Feuilleloop was said to be the most fearful woman in Quilli, possibly the most fearful woman in Maine, and maybe even the most fearful woman on all of the earth. No one questioned if there was a reason for this. Fears are private, all agreed, something like sexual feelings or the ways in which some people wonder if they are truly going to die.

Besides, Elsie Feuilleloop would talk to no one. Her house was kept shut and locked, the storm windows on, and the curtains pulled summer and winter. People wondered about the air in her house.

The manager of Don's Grocery delivered food to her house at seven o'clock every Sunday evening but he had never seen her. They billed her, he said, and the money was always in the store mail by noon on Tuesday: cash, Canadian, calculated to the exact exchange rate.

Thus, it was assumed Elsie Feuilleloop wasn't dead.

ELSIE FEUILLELOOP ASSUMED SHE wasn't dead, too, but it was something to think about. She had a big leg and for a long time she waited for the swelling to go down before she'd go out in public. That attitude lasted—she was not much concerned about dates or times—for ten years.

She'd had a big compost box in her backyard and she'd been forking the weeds and leaves and grass clippings from one side to the other when she'd fallen down to one leg. Something had either stuck or bitten her because the leg had swollen up, from calf to thigh, in about a week. The swelling was pretty consistently the width of a basketball.

She had no relatives and no one else, in her opinion, worth talking to so her oddity could not be dispersed by conversation the way it often is in small towns. It didn't hurt either so there was no reason to go to the doctor. People in Quilli tend not to seek treatment if there isn't any pain.

IN THE ELEVENTH YEAR of this strangeness, so it was said (this was the 1930s), there was an eruption on her big leg. It had taken time but finally, she was sure, the poison was being drawn out.

Not exactly.

The pustule was, indeed, that, gray and green and blue and puffy, but it didn't burst and yetch all over with the kind of stuff no one dared touch. Instead —she kept diaries so this is not all conjecture—it sprouted. It was a point at first, a sprout, a seedling. Then it bloomed.

ELSIE'S FASCINATION WITH THIS was complete. Childless, even in her youth, she wrote: *Fertility! Amazing! It is as though I were blossoming from the still empty grave!*

She was not a prolific diarist, nor was she a recorder of feelings and moods, and all of her entries were written on Don's Grocery wrapping paper neatly trimmed to an 8½-by-11-inch size.

An inch, if anything, the color of sweet lime. I have taken to opening one curtain for the morning sun.

Some have said it must have been like mothering a cancer.

Two inches! Clearly, the most delicate of needles. Like some gentle varicosity, I begin to see its roots just beneath my skin.

Joy gives no quarter to horror. Elsie writes of "this

child" living to be two hundred years old, of its standing up to all manner of storms, floods, and great snows. Rhapsodically, she imagines fine treaties being signed beneath its branches (with no mention of the sort of conflicts those treaties would be resolving). Not so much the spinster as the hermit, she writes of lovers shaded by its boughs and frankly, too: *sweet sex and all the joyous juice of youth.*

"My God!" however, one wag opined, "a simple pluck and the whole damn leg would have returned to normal."

Normal, of course, had not been part of Elsie Feuilleloop for a long time.

Six inches! But I fear it drains me in strenuous measure. Wouldst seem I am not earth enough.

Beyond that, there was only the will: butcher paper, durable ink. There was to be no service and no casket and the proceeds from her estate were to go to the town. For the rest, no one knows. Was she buried upside down? Was that leg removed from her body? Small towns lose all of that in time.

There is a stone, however, at the cemetery, the old

one right near the center of town. It reads ELSIE FEUILLELOOP, A FEARFUL WOMAN, though it's not easy to read, the face of the stone being only inches from a gorgeous and easily sixty-foot-tall pine tree.

LAUGHTER

There is an old-town part of Quilli, as there is in so many Maine towns, that has always sat like some urban bastard seeking respect and just a little money. It is down the hill off State Street, behind the warehouses, runs with two short curves of the river, and is mainly two taverns (Le Père's and Bud's), an unaffiliated hardware store, a house with rooms to rent, and other houses variously rented, bought, sold, occasionally abandoned.

At times old town has been built up new to look old, and at other times built up old to look new. Enough money has been lost trying to make it a tourist stop that the street in old town has been jokingly called Debtor's Way.

The sages call it a mud mall and say don't even try to pound survival out of an old river.

The bards say it is an enchanting area; it is quirky

ambience, a link to a heritage of smoky nights and the shriek of tree creatures—history's trellis all bent over with moldy weeds and the secrets of lean, tough people.

The bards are always the wordier bunch.

AS THE PLACE DECEIVES, so sometimes do the words. Michelle Monelle was a businesswoman, her business modest even by old town's open standards. She ran a taxi company from the back booth in Bud's Bar. Larger companies came and went in Quilli, always trying to pull more business out of the cab market than was there, but Michelle Monelle kept rolling along with her one small ad in the yellow pages, her record book and phone in the booth at Bud's, and her 1974 Oldsmobile Cutlass Supreme out on the street.

Some said that old Oldsmobile was the newest thing in old town.

MICHELLE HAD BEEN MARRIED to Bud once, but like many marriages where partners are chosen from a limited pool, they both looked at each other one day and said, "Who *are* you?" and that was that. Bud took the tavern and Michelle got the car, each convinced of having got the better deal.

They slept with each other maybe once a week because that was easier than dating. Michelle had a lot of energy in the sexual area and Bud didn't, although Bud was an excellent cook and liked feeding Michelle. As anyone can be over small things, Bud was proud of the marble rolling pin he'd bought one time in North Conway over in New Hampshire. It was as big around as a good softball and he used it mostly to make his famous shredded beef hamburgers.

He also used it one night to save Michelle's life. This is what everyone believes.

MICHELLE KNEW, SHE SAYS, that the fellow from New York was not going to be a good fare. He told her he was up there for a business deal—a prospect that always stands out in Quilli—but she also said he was drunk and was carrying a gun and kept asking her how far it was to the Canadian border and would she take him there.

She said no, it was too complicated doing business in Canada, even something as simple as a cab fare, and why didn't he rent a car?

Why didn't she just climb back into the Porta-John she'd crawled out of was what he told her.

By this time she was parked in front of Bud's and ready to tell the man he was on his own when he reached over and put his hand on her breast and began treating it, as she said, like it was a bag of whole wheat flour he was trying to get off a store shelf.

"That's not the door handle," she told him. His hand moved then from her breast down between her legs, the action there she said like that of a cold man trying to wiggle into a good mitten.

Later, she told the police he might have thought she was encouraging him when she leaned into him hard, putting her whole chest in his face, but all she was doing was leaning over to open his door so that when she finally got her pepper spray off the visor overhead he'd be able to find a quick exit from her car, her life, and all that a quiet place like Quilli has to offer.

In truth, he pulled on her and she thought it was like a fight, especially the way her feet and legs flew all around inside that big car, her feet just missing Bud's face, who'd heard there was a fracas in front and who'd stepped outside with his marble rolling pin.

So she and the man, Bud said, tumbled out of the car. Michelle was belly up and feet first as she landed on the street with her head under the car. As Bud started to help Michelle, the man tumbled out, too, and ended up lying next to Michelle with Bud thinking this wasn't so much a reason for Michelle to get out of the cab business as it was for the airport to shut down.

"Speaking of shutting down, though," he went on, "the car started to roll, slow as you want but backward toward Michelle's head and you just don't know what to do."

Which, as he said, was how Michelle's cheekbone got broken because there were only inches between her head and the tire when Bud slammed his marble rolling pin from North Conway down onto the street and onto her cheek and under the wheel, with a lot of other things going on, too.

He said the untrustworthy guy was squirming around under the car like a stuck bug until he, Bud, trying to pull Michelle out, could see that the man was—Bud's words—"packing a rod," so that with Michelle free and sitting up on the sidewalk, her anger a greater pain than the numb bone in her cheek, Bud said he was ready to unload a week's groceries but all he could think of was to grab his marble rolling pin from North Conway and see if this guy was having a good day or not.

"NOT," BUD SAYS. "OR maybe. He didn't die."

There was a loud "Oh," though, from the dozen people by then outside the bar as the Oldsmobile tire rolled into the man's face.

"It was his general head, I suppose," Bud said, "that stopped the car."

But the pressure on his face, on his skin, Bud said, must have been awful. They had to leave him there— thinking it was safer for all concerned—for about twenty minutes until the Quilli night-shift cop could get down there.

With the night-shift cop there they pushed the Oldsmobile forward enough to free the man (although Michelle accidentally kicked him as she leaned in fast through the door to jam the gear into Park). They got the man up on his feet then and again there was a group "Oh" as they saw his face, saw the brow skin and the cheek skin and the chin skin all pulled and stretched so that it hung down almost to his chest.

"Grotesque," Bud said, "but everything was all over now and the night-shift cop knew the right things to do and you know there was a laugh, and then another laugh, and before you knew it everyone was howling."

IT WAS HARD TO tell, he said, if there was justice in that laugh, or humor, or relief or what, but you can be laughed at in Quilli, he said, no matter what your trouble or your problem, so long as you're being helped. "That's the key," he said, "so long as you're being helped.

"So it was okay."